BETRAYED
BY *Lies*

REBECCA SHEA

BETRAYED
BY *Lies*

REBECCA SHEA

COPYRIGHT

Edited by: Megan Hand, Story Girl Editing and Julie Deaton

dedication

To those that never gave up on Sam.
This is for you.

PROLOGUE

18 MONTHS AGO

I've learned from experience that distraction can get you killed, and that's what I've been—distracted.

A shadow slips past me as I grip the steering wheel and blink my eyes. Before I even hear the gunshots, I see bursts of light and hear glass shattering before I feel the pressure.

One.

Two.

Three.

I feel all three shards of metal pierce my chest, and I gasp for breath. I glance down and see blood staining my shirt.

The shadow approaches, and this time I see his face—Saul Trujillo. He lifts his gun one last time and pulls the trigger, hitting me in the chest again. Four. I count the number of bullets that have hit me and gasp for air as he sprints away. Four pieces of metal ripped through my flesh. My body is shrouded in warmth, yet I'm paralyzed from shock. I panic when the light from the open front door spills into the darkness around me.

Emilia. Her long hair dances in the air as she runs down the steps of my front porch.

The panic.

The screaming.

The fear in her eyes.

I see it all, yet I close my eyes, trying to block it out.

"Sam!" she screams at me, bringing me back to her. My eyes scan her slowly. "Sam. God, no." She yanks on the handle, but the doors are locked. With a shaky hand, she reaches through the broken glass and presses the lock release, yanking the door open, desperately trying to get to me. Reaching across me, she pulls my cell phone from the center console and frantically presses the screen, finally screaming into the phone.

Crying.

Tears.

Begging.

She pleads with someone on the other end of the phone to send help before her pleas turn to me. "Sam, stay with me. You can't leave me," she begs me.

I feel myself slipping away, and my heart aches that I pulled Emilia into this mess. If I could go back and do it over, I would. I wish I could tell her this. My lips move, but I can't speak. I try to clear my throat, but I'm tired. I know I'm losing blood and slowly losing consciousness.

Emilia holds my head in her soft hands. "Look at me, Sam. Help is coming. Stay with me, okay?"

I blink once and try to nod. Forcing myself to get her information, I'm able to finally muster out, "Saul."

"Saul did this?" She feverishly glances around, and I want to tell her to run, she shouldn't be here.

I nod and try to swallow.

"Sam, don't talk. Just stay with me." She presses her hand to my chest, and I can feel her body shaking against me. "Stay with me," she whispers. "Help is coming. I can hear the sirens.

Do you hear them? They're close." She tries to remain calm, but I can see the fear in her eyes, her beautiful eyes. They should be twinkling and dancing in the moonlight, full of laughter. Instead, they're full of fear and panic as she pleads with me to stay with her.

Emilia. Sweet Emilia.

ONE

Sam

I wake with a start, sitting straight up in my bed. Cool air fills my lungs when I gasp, pulling a deep breath in. My eyes slowly adjust to the dark room, and I rub the sweat from my forehead before swinging my feet over the edge of the bed and resting my arms on my knees. The dream is always the same, the piercing pain of the bullets hitting my flesh...and the fear of dying, scared and alone.

An exaggerated huff leaves my mouth when I see the alarm clock on the bedside table. It reads four-ten in the morning. That puts three hours and twenty minutes of sleep under my belt. It's the longest I've slept since I arrived in Los Angeles three days ago.

I'm used to surviving on very little sleep, but the nightmares of that night are back and making it more difficult to find rest. I push myself out of bed and throw on a pair of athletic shorts and t-shirt. Grabbing my phone and hotel room key, I head to the gym. With no one else up this early, I play music directly from my phone while watching CNN with subtitles as I get my daily seven-mile run in.

I like running outdoors better, but it's easier to use the gym and treadmill here at the hotel. My phone pings with incoming texts, but I focus on my run. The burn in my lungs relieves the stress in my shoulders. Sweat coats my skin and drips from my nose as I increase my speed—pushing myself harder. The treadmill roars as I increase the speed yet again, and my heart pounds wildly against my ribcage as my lungs fight for air.

Pain—it's the only way I know I'm alive.

Pain in my chest. My mind. My body.

The treadmill slows just as my phone pings again, multiple times, alerting me to more incoming text messages—messages that I ignore. I've got three days' worth waiting for a response, and I'm in no hurry to get to them. Transferring to the ATF offices in Los Angeles makes for an easy reason to avoid everyone and everything. Avoidance is what I do best.

I grab a bottle of water and return to my room for a shower before heading into my new office. New office. New job. New city. New state. New life.

A chance to start over. A chance to leave the past where it belongs…in the past. I pull a suit out of the closet and turn on the shower to let the water warm up.

Raking my hands over my face, I do my best to shove the events of last year to the back of my mind, but the life goes out of my eyes when I see the scars scattered across my chest. They're a constant reminder of the day I lost almost everything…including my life.

Standing in front of the mirror, I run my hand up over my chest and shoulder, my fingertips brushing the smooth surface of the scars spread across the left side of my chest. I ball my hands tightly and release, repeating two more times, a coping mechanism my therapist taught me to deal with my anger.

I step into the shower and let the hot water ease my tension.

My neck, shoulders, and back instantly begin to relax, and I allow my mind to let go at the same time. "New beginnings," I mumble to myself as the shower cleanses me of my anger, a baptism of sorts.

I dress and am out the door in less than thirty minutes, easing my car onto the bumper-to-bumper packed L.A. freeway. A commute that would take me less than ten minutes in Phoenix takes me damn near forty-five here. I find a covered parking spot just as my phone begins to ring. A number I don't recognize flashes on the screen, and I decline the call. I don't have the time nor patience to deal with unknown callers. Gathering my suit coat and phone, I find my way to the main entrance, using the security badge that was sent to me prior to my arrival to allow me entrance into the building.

My phone begins ringing again just as I'm weaving my way through the lobby and headed to the elevators. Same number. This time I press accept and answer. Before I even speak, the female voice on the other end catches me off guard.

"Oh my god, I didn't expect you to answer." She pauses. "I was leaving a voice mail and my call dropped so I was just calling back to finish the message." I hear her sigh. "This is Kate Stevens. Nick Stevens sister. He gave me your number." Nick Stevens, my new boss. "He mentioned that you might need a place to rent. I have a guesthouse he thought would be perfect for you, and he asked me to call you. I'm sorry if this caught you off guard. He said he was going to speak with you." She finally stops speaking so I can get a word in.

"Hello, Kate. Nick didn't mention this to me."

I hear her sigh loudly. "He's the most unorganized human being alive," she mumbles, and I can't help but chuckle. I've met the guy three times, and she's right from my observation as well. "I'm so sorry to have called you," she apologizes.

"Don't be. I'd love to check out the place. I got here Friday, and I've been staying in a hotel while I look for something more permanent—"

"Don't feel obligated," she cuts me off.

"I don't," I answer her honestly. "I'm mainly looking for something not too far from the office and just somewhere to lay my head. Nothing fancy. I won't be around much because all I ever do is work."

"Sounds like Nick," she says with a small laugh. "You're welcome to check out the house anytime. It's close to your office, but it's a little off the beaten path near the foothills. Either call or text me, and we'll schedule a time for you to stop by, or have Nick show it to you anytime. He knows where I hide the spare key. I'm also not home often so coordinating our schedules might be tough."

I hear a horn honk in the background as she mutters a string of curse words worthy of an R-rating, and I can't help but laugh. "That sounds great. Thanks for calling, Kate."

She ends the call without another word, and I'm left standing in the lobby of my new office, laughing.

The morning is spent being briefed on projects that the team is working on and investigating. I'll be taking over a case that my predecessor left when he was promoted to a position in Washington D.C., as well as anything new that comes in.

There's a quick knock on my doorjamb before Nick sticks his head in my office. "You got any lunch plans?"

"Not today," I toss over my shoulder as I close the folder on my desk.

"Let's go grab a quick bite. I need to get the hell out of this office." He loosens the tie around his neck. Nick is about my height and build, probably a few years older than me, California born and raised, and started in the San Diego field office. Worked his way up to Los Angeles and plans to retire here.

I grab my phone and slide it into the pocket of my suit jacket.

"How's the first day treating you?" he asks as we weave through cubicles lining the rectangular office floor outside our offices.

"Good. Just briefing myself on the Navarro case."

"We've been working on that for years," he grumbles. "Hoping you can close the deal on that one." His car beeps as we approach and he unlocks the doors. "Hey," he buckles himself in and starts the car. "You do great work. I heard how you took down the Estrada cartel." He slides his sunglasses on his face.

My heart races as I wonder how much he knows—if he's aware the Estradas are my family. It was well known in the Phoenix office, but I'm not sure how much Los Angeles knows about my 'family' history. I nod but don't say anything.

"You're the best of the best, which is why you're going to take down Navarro," he continues as we take off down the road. "It was easy for me to approve the transfer request."

"Thanks." I offer a tight smile and turn to look out the passenger window.

"I'm excited for you to kick ass here in L.A. So why the hell did you want to leave Phoenix anyway? There's so much shit going on in that office, you must've had years of work still."

I blow a puff of air from my mouth. "My injuries—"

"Shit, I forgot about that. Sorry, continue." He winces.

"My injuries have fully healed with time and physical therapy, and I wrapped up the cases I was working on." I look at him out of the corner of my eye to gauge his response. He raps his thumb against the steering wheel and nods his head slowly.

"And it just felt like it was a good time to start fresh. Start over with a clean slate."

He turns his head to look at me. "I cannot tell you how lucky we are to have you here in Los Angeles. I hope you're fully prepared to kick ass and take names."

I can't help but smile, appreciating the vote of confidence.

As the day winds down and the office empties, I find myself wrapped up in the case file on my desk, familiarizing myself with all the key players, the locations where the guns are being held, and the evidence that we have to date, along with notes on what we still need to document.

Nick doesn't knock when he enters my office this time, rather throwing himself into the chair across my desk with an exaggerated sigh.

"What's the sigh for?" I ask him as I tuck the case file into my bag. I'll finish combing through the remaining details tonight and make my own notes. I have a system for how I set up my case folders, and I need to rework all of these.

"Just a Monday," he states, looking around my bare office. "You going to decorate or something? Throw a poster on the wall?" He waves his hand around, gesturing to the stark gray walls.

"Decorate? No. I do have some awards and diplomas I'll hang once they arrive. They're being sent from Phoenix."

He nods, content with that answer.

I clear my throat. "Speaking of decorating, I got a call from Kate." I raise my eyebrows and sit back in my desk chair. "She said something about having a guesthouse to rent. Were you going to tell me she was going to call?"

"I did. I sent you a text on Saturday." He relaxes in his chair and props a foot on his opposite knee. I really need to stop ignoring my messages. He continues, "I stopped by to see her this weekend and forgot she had that guesthouse. Immediately thought of you when I saw it."

"Thanks. I need to find some time to check it out. Living out of a hotel room is less than ideal." I reach over and power down my laptop.

"Let's go now. It's just down the road a few miles. I know where she keeps the spare key if she's not there."

"She also mentioned that," I laugh.

"Grab your shit and let's go. You can follow me there." He jumps up from the chair and quickly pulls his tie off. Nick looks more like an outdoorsman than a senior agent with the ATF. He looks uncomfortable in a suit. I see him more as the park ranger type, running around in cargos and hiking boots.

I follow suit, loosening my tie as I follow him to our cars.

A few miles is more like fifteen, and about half of those miles are in bumper-to-bumper L.A. traffic. Something that I'm not sure I'll ever adjust to. Once we exit the freeway, we wind through gorgeous neighborhoods all the way back to the base of the foothills. I would never in a million years guess the house we pull up to is a house in a suburb of Los Angeles. It sits on what I assume is about an acre of lush green land with neighbors spread out down a long secluded, tree-lined street. The ranch style house is simple yet modern with an updated exterior, wood shutters, and wrought iron accessories.

"Not a bad drive, eh," Nick says as we both step out of our cars in the driveway. "I should say for L.A. standards. If your commute is under an hour, you're pretty much living the life," he laughs.

It really wasn't a bad commute. I eyeball the watch on my

wrist and the drive was just under thirty minutes. Nick reaches inside a hanging planter that swings from the covered front porch and pulls out a key. He waves me toward the side of the house where a brick sidewalk snakes around to the guesthouse that sits just off the main house. It looks exactly like the main house, just slightly smaller.

"This is it," he says, sliding the key into the front door. "One bedroom, a small office slash library, kitchen, living room, and one and a half baths."

We step inside. It's obviously been remodeled recently. The smell of fresh paint hits me as I walk deeper into the house. Everything is brand new, sleek, and modern. Bright white trim and doors offset light gray walls. A dark wood floor makes the bright white kitchen pop against the stainless steel appliances.

"The only thing that's missing is a washer and dryer. She said she'd order those once she leased the house. The laundry room is off the back." He points to a door off the kitchen. "It's a large pantry and a laundry room."

I'm impressed with what I've seen thus far. I walk through the open living room and down the hall to the bedroom. It's large and bright with one wall of windows that start near the ceiling and stretch about three quarters of the way down the wall. Long, dark gray curtains hang to each side of the paneled windows that overlooks more of the lush backyard. There's a single French door that leads to a small brick patio off the master bedroom, and a table and chairs sit out there. In the middle of the table is a fire pit. I instantly imagine myself relaxing around this table with a beer after a long day at the office.

I head back down the hallway where I stop and peek my head in the office. It's got two glass French doors that lead into the square room. One entire wall has built in bookshelves and a built in desk. It's the perfect home office.

I scan the living room and kitchen again and make note that my dark furniture will fit perfectly in the space and complements the gray and white theme throughout. This might be the easiest decision I've made since deciding to move to Los Angeles.

Nick steps out front while I take one last look around, making mental notes of the space and things I'll need shipped from Phoenix.

After we step outside and Nick locks the door, I hear him shuffling behind me on the brick walkway. "So what do you think?"

"Perfect. It's everything I was looking for," I say as I spin around and am met face-to-face with the bluest eyes I've ever seen. I stumble momentarily because, for half a second, those words mean so much more than just the house I was looking at.

"I'm Kate," she says, her voice strong and secure. She holds her hand out to shake mine. She's tall with light brown hair that hangs just past her shoulders, and she's wearing a navy blue dress and heels that put her at almost my six-foot-two. Confident. She's confident. I can read a woman by the way she carries herself, the tone of her voice, and what she wears.

I take her hand in mine and smile. "Sam. Sam Cortez. I'll take it." Again, those words mean so much more than just the house.

Her lips turn into a half smile, and she holds eye contact with me. She licks her lips and tilts her head before glancing over to Nick and then back to me. "Nice to meet you, Sam Cortez. Welcome home."

And my heart begins to beat again for the first time in eighteen months.

TWO

Kate

"What do you mean you rented out your guesthouse?" Adam asks as he rests his butt on the side of my desk. "You always said you like being alone. You like the privacy and the quiet." His fingers grip the edge of my desk, and his dark brown eyes narrow a bit as he interrogates me. Adam is my best friend and coworker. I don't know what I'd do without him—even when he's bossy and controlling and bugs the hell out of me.

I shrug and sit back in my chair. "I don't know," I answer him softly. "I'm rarely there, so why not make some money off the back house. It was remodeled when they did the main house and now just seems like a good time to rent it."

"That really puts a wrinkle in your plan to live a solitary life with eighty-seven cats," he says sarcastically. I swat his arm. He feigns hurt but laughs at me.

"I hate cats." I roll my eyes at him.

"So who's the lucky renter? Your house is gorgeous and that yard…" He whistles. "It really is a great place, Kate. Just tell me you didn't rent it to someone off of Craigslist or one of those other sites. You know that's where mass murderers look for their victims, right? You're the classic case. Lonely career woman. Lives on the outskirts of town. Very few friends or family to check on her. I'm telling you, this person could off you."

I swat at him again.

"Or, God, please don't tell me you rented it to some frat boy who's going to have parties and fuck it up. Are you a cougar, Kate?" Adam looks ten years younger than his thirty-nine-year-old self, and his face pulls into a giant smile as he teases me.

"Adam!" I yell at him, and he hunches away from me.

He bends over laughing, and I glare at him. "I'm just sayin'." He raises his hands in surrender. "But for real, Kate. You have like two friends. You work all the time, which makes the rest of us look bad by the way...And who is this new roommate anyway?"

I raise my eyebrows and school him. "First. I have more than two friends, and second, he works for the ATF with my brother. So he's been properly background checked and has a stable job. It's a win-win."

"Rebuttal," he says, sitting up straighter and squaring his shoulders. It's what he does when he knows he's losing an argument. It makes him appear bigger, more confident. "One. You do have only two friends. Me and Kandi. And for the record, I've never met Kandi, so you might only have one friend —" He points to himself with a grin. "—me. Plus, anyone that spells their name Kandi with a K is probably working the pole at some seedy strip joint and only calls you on Tuesdays when she's not working."

"You're a dick," I grumble at him.

He smirks, a cocky grin spreading across his face. "We've already established this."

"Kandi is a stay-at-home mom who rarely has time to pee, let alone work the pole or meet me out for wine nights or club hopping, not that I do that at this age anyway." My clubbing days are long gone. That ship sailed years ago. I should be married, having kids, starting the 'next chapter' of my life, but instead of settling down with a man, I've settled into corporate life—and while I love my job, I'm lonely.

His shoulders fall. "I'm sorry, Kate. I'm just giving you a hard time, but seriously, this is shocking news coming from you. You're just so 'Kate'," he says softly. "You don't like people in your space, and I just feel like this decision is really sudden." He pauses, looking hurt. "And you didn't discuss it with me."

I blow a puff of air from my lips, causing them to make a sound. "You're my friend, not my mother. And it's a rental agreement, Adam. Not an arranged marriage. It's a smart business decision, and it'll be nice to have someone else living on the property."

"There's more to this story, Kate Stevens." His tone changes, and he winks at me as he pushes himself up from my desk. Adam starts walking away, but looks back over his shoulder to see if I'm going to respond.

"There's not," I holler at him. "Mark my words."

"Noted!" he says, laughing as he turns the corner and heads down the hall to his office. I pull up a contract I'm reviewing on my screen and get to work. Life as a corporate attorney is far from glamorous, but it's busy and it keeps my loneliness at bay.

I finally give up and shut down my computer for the day. The sun is just setting, and I'm feeling tired. I've been too easily distracted today, and I'm pretty sure it's the golden brown eyes and big smile that met me yesterday and will be moving into my guesthouse.

Nick startled me when I arrived home yesterday, but what startled me more was my instant attraction to Sam. Something in his eyes spoke to me without him saying a single word. He was tall with sun-kissed skin and golden brown eyes, far from what I was expecting to see when Nick told me his newest transfer Sam Cortez needed a place to rent.

I was expecting a middle aged balding ATF agent, not a fit, attractive man that you'd find on the beaches with a surfboard pressed to his side. His tailored suit hugged every muscle, and when he smiled his cheek formed the perfect dimple.

Taking a breath, I try to shake the thoughts of Sam from my head as I head to the elevators.

"Well, well, well...." I can hear the smile in Adam's voice when he sidles up next to me at the elevator. "Someone is leaving early tonight." He rocks back and forth from his toes to his heels as we wait for the elevator to arrive.

I want to smile at him calling me out, but I won't give him the satisfaction. "I always work late. I can leave on time today." I give him the side eyes.

He wraps his arm around my shoulder and pulls me into the elevator with him.

"It's like I don't even know you anymore, Kate. What happened to my best friend?" he chides.

"She's still here. Just tired," I sigh.

"Are you still getting those headaches?" he asks, the conversation taking a more serious turn. His eyes search mine with concern.

"Sometimes. The doctor said not to worry, that it was probably just stress. He told me to relax and not work so hard," I chuckle and roll my eyes. I don't divulge that the doctor wants me to have an MRI, or that he's concerned with how intense the headaches have grown so suddenly.

"Well, then, I'm glad you're leaving on time tonight." He nudges me with his shoulder.

"Me, too." I smile at Adam. He's been my best friend since I started working here ten years ago. He's a confidant and a source of constant entertainment for me, but more importantly, he genuinely looks out for me—no strings attached. He and I were inseparable until he met his now wife, Melissa. Our relationship has always been platonic, caring for each other in the brother-sister sense and nothing more.

"Are you able to grab lunch this week?" he asks as we walk to our cars.

"Yep. Block some time on my calendar." Adam and I have access to each other's calendars and often block time on each other's calendars just so we can catch up.

"I will. Have a good night, Katie. Relax and have some wine." He's the only person other than Nick that's allowed to call me Katie. I hate that name. I'm Kate. I've always been Kate. But for those two men, I give them a pass.

"I plan to! Say hi to Melissa and kiss that sweet little boy of yours for me, will ya?"

"Oh, you know I will." He grins at me.

Like I do most nights, I stop for takeout and bring it home to eat. Only most nights I continue to work while I eat, but tonight I'm taking the night off. I eat my Chinese takeout straight out of the containers on my back patio. The late summer air is bringing in slightly cooler nights, and there's a breeze that provides just enough movement to almost cause a chill.

Unwinding on my oversized outdoor chaise lounge that overlooks the pool, a blanket pulled over my legs, I finish my Kung Pao shrimp over rice and sip on a glass of chilled Pinot Grigio.

I glance across the yard to the guesthouse and wonder when

Sam plans to move in. I emailed him a lease agreement but haven't heard back, so I make a mental note to follow up in a couple of days if I don't hear before then.

Collecting my trash and the blanket, I head inside for the night. A bubble bath and a book will make this evening complete. My phone chimes, but I choose to ignore it, most likely work that can definitely wait until tomorrow.

Running a hot bath, I toss a bath bomb in the water and twist my hair into a bun on top of my head. Slinking into the hot water, my body and mind start to fully relax. Thoughts of Sam swim through my head, but I push him to the side, reminding myself that this is a professional relationship. He's a tenant. Nothing more. He's also Nick's employee, another reminder that this will never be anything more than a business relationship.

With that in mind, I finish my bath. When I'm done, I pull the plug and watch the water drain, along with any thoughts that Sam Cortez could be anything more than my tenant.

My alarm clock startles me and I hit snooze, which is totally unlike me. I'm professional, put together, and always on time. Always. Except today I'm exhausted. It took me hours to fall asleep last night as thoughts of Sam danced through my head. I doze back to sleep until I swear I hear my doorbell ringing. I manage to open one eye, and the clock reads seven o'clock in the morning. Panicked, I fly out of bed and down the hallway, not considering that I'm wearing nothing more than a thin white camisole and sleep shorts.

I fling the door open just as those same golden eyes I dreamt about meet mine for the second time this week. Only this time his eyes grow wide and his smile fades.

"I take it now is a bad time?" he says quietly, stepping away from me.

"Huh?" I ask, confused and still in a sleep induced stupor.

"To drop off the lease, but I had some questions…" He nervously twists a small stack of papers, presumably the lease, in his hands. "I sent you a text message last night. I said I'd stop by before work in the morning unless I heard from you not to." He tries to keep his eyes focused on mine, but I see them drop to my chest and then lower to my bare legs. I try to hide myself as best I can behind the large front door, but it's mostly glass and see-through so I'm doing a terrible job.

"I'll come back." He takes another few steps backward. "Tonight."

"I'm so sorry," I apologize, knowing what a mess I must look like. "I overslept."

He smirks.

"And I wasn't prepared for anyone—"

"Obviously. I'll come back tonight. What time is good?"

I can't even think straight. My heart is racing, and I'm doing my best to keep my composure. "I'll text you when I have a better idea."

"I'll be waiting." He turns on a heel and walks away, but not before glancing one last time over his shoulder with a grin on his face. I close the door and press my back against it, replaying the last twenty seconds and wanting to crawl into a hole and die.

"Kate, you need to get the hell out of here," Adam says, adjusting the strap of his computer case on his shoulder just outside my office door.

I'm frantically responding to one of our international

attorneys regarding a foreign business acquisition. "You're still here, too," I remark and sigh loudly.

"Come on. Shut down. I'll walk you out." I sit back in my chair and tip my head backward, inhaling a deep breath.

"Okay," I give in. With fall just around the corner, it's getting darker earlier and the sun has already set, making it feel later than seven-thirty in the evening.

"I'm worried about you," Adam says quietly as he leans against the doorframe. "You work too much. You need a life, Kate." He raises his eyebrows at me sympathetically.

"You work too much, too," I counter quickly. "You have a wife and baby at home. I have nothing." There's a hint of sadness in my response.

"You don't have nothing, Kate, but you need to get out more. Spend more time with Nick and his family. You lost your parents, your only sibling lives less than forty minutes away, and you maybe see him twice a year, and that's if he comes to see you." Adam is a straight shooter. He'll tell you the hard stuff, but he does it with love and sincerity.

"Look," he continues. "I was so happy you left early yesterday. I thought maybe you'd go home and set up a match-dot-com profile or something. You need to get out. You need a boyfriend."

I raise my eyebrows at him and purse my lips. "I don't need—"

"You do, Kate."

I let out another loud sigh, not wanting to argue with my best friend.

"Come over next weekend. We're going to barbecue. I'm going to have some friends from college over. Just come have a few drinks, relax." He waits for me to answer, and from the look on his face, he won't be taking 'no' as an answer.

I smile at him. "I will. That actually sounds fun."

"No work this weekend, promise?" he pleads with me.

"No work."

"Atta girl. Now let's go." He smirks.

I shove my laptop in my oversized purse and meet Adam at the door. He loops his arm through mine, and we walk through the dimly lit office.

"Why are we such overachievers?" he questions when he sees the empty office. Our coworkers cleared out hours ago. He nudges me with his shoulder and we laugh together.

"Because that's what we do," I respond sarcastically with an eye roll.

THREE

My phone pings, alerting me to an incoming text message. I pull myself away from the research I'm doing on a new case and reach for my phone.

Kate: I'm home. Sorry about this morning. If this is too late, we can schedule another time to meet.

I glance at the clock on my office wall, and it's just after eight in the evening. It's time for me to get the hell out of this office anyway, so I quickly respond.

Me: Was just leaving work. Can be there in about thirty minutes.

Kate: See you when you get here.

I shut down for the evening and lock my office. It's been a long two days, and I'm not taking work back to the hotel with me tonight—there's nothing that can't wait until tomorrow. I rub my eyes and gather my belongings, along with the lease for Kate.

It's unbelievable to me that at nearly eight-thirty there is still insane traffic on the L.A. freeways. I tap the steering wheel as I coast slowly toward the exit that will take me to Kate's house and my new home. A little after nine o'clock, I roll up the dark, tree-lined street, winding my way to the foothills. The only illumination comes from coach lights hung on houses and dim streetlights strategically placed every quarter mile along the neighborhood street. It's quiet, dark, and peaceful. It's perfect and calming, and I can't wait to move here.

I park and follow the lighted walkway up the middle of the front yard to the large glass door. Reaching for the doorbell, I pause when I see Kate standing in her living room. A glass of wine in one hand and her other hand brushing the spines of books on the bookshelf.

Her light brown hair with blonde highlights is piled loosely on top of her head, while a few long pieces that have fallen dance around her shoulders. With her lips pursed, her forehead wrinkles slightly as she studies each book carefully. Her toned curves are easy to see through the tank top and leggings she's wearing. Firm, lightly tanned skin peeks out just above the waistband of her leggings where her tank top rides up, and I wonder what it would feel like to brush my fingers across the span of her skin. All of it, not just her waist. My cock hardens in my pants, causing an ache in my belly.

Shaking the thoughts of Kate naked from my mind, I reach for the doorbell. The last thing I need is to look like a creep staring at her through the front door. I press the button and take a step back as I turn my attention to the dark sky. You can see every star out here, almost every constellation.

I hear the front door swing open, and I drop my head to find Kate smiling at me, a welcoming smile.

"Sam," she says my name like I'm an old friend. "Please, come in." She takes a step back and holds the door open.

"I hope it's not too late," I muster as I step over the threshold and into the main living area. An instant hominess overtakes me. Large plush couches are positioned facing each other, each of them piled high with pillows, blankets draping each arm. A large wall houses a library full of books and picture frames highlighting her interests. Everything is neat and clean, yet simple and livable—it seems so, perfectly Kate.

"It's not too late." She shuts the door behind us. "I apologize for not being home sooner, work has been—"

"Crazy. For me, too," I cut her off. "Don't apologize. I just have a couple of questions for you before I sign the lease." I hold up the small stack of papers that comprise the rental agreement. I've never seen something so thorough and detailed.

"Sure." She moves closer to me, putting herself mere inches away. My heart races as she closes the distance, and her scent surrounds me. Our shoulders brush as I thumb through the document looking for the page I have questions on. I can smell the lightest hints of floral perfume that lingers on her skin, and I want to rub my nose and lips down the curve of her neck.

"Here." I find it and set it on top of the stack. "The agreement doesn't specifically state anything about an alarm." I look up at her. "Obviously, working with Nick, you would know that, at times, I have sensitive information with me, along with several firearms. I'd like to have an alarm system installed, at my expense, and will leave it here when I eventually vacate the premises."

She looks up at me quickly, her eyes narrowing in confusion.

Hastily, I add, "I'm fulfilling the full terms of the lease, I just mean I won't have the system removed once I eventually leave."

She nods her head and smiles. "I have no problem with that. Let me redraft that section and get you a new copy to sign." Now I look at her like she's crazy, and she smiles politely at me.

"Sorry. It's the lawyer in me. Everything in writing is my motto…makes it legally binding."

I nod at her. "Understood."

"Is there anything else you wanted me to amend?" She reaches for the current lease, pulling it gently from my hand, and then she folds it before tearing it in half and walking over to her laptop that's sitting on an end table.

I shake my head. "No, that should be it."

"Great. Give me just a minute and I'll get you a new copy." She pulls a pair of glasses off the table, sliding them onto her face before she begins clicking away at the keyboard. It's impossible not to notice how beautiful she is. Her eyes squint just a little, and her lips purse as she concentrates on the task in front of her. The strands of long hair hanging down over her shoulders, resting just atop her perfectly round breasts.

"There's beer in the fridge if you want one while you wait," she says, her fingers gliding across the computer. "Or wine. There's an open bottle on the island. Glasses are in the cabinet above the fridge."

I don't hesitate at Kate's offer, pulling open the fridge door and finding a shelf half-full of beer. I pull a Stella out of the fridge when I notice all the takeout boxes, which look oddly familiar, like my refrigerator back in Phoenix before I cleaned it out prior to my move here.

"Bottle opener is in the drawer to the left of the fridge," she hollers as if she's reading my mind.

"Thanks," I answer, finding the bottle opener right on top of the contents in the drawer. Opening the beer, I lean against the counter as I continue watching her type away. The muscles in her long arms flex as she types, accentuating her feminine figure. Lean, but soft.

The taste of ice-cold beer rolling over my tongue and down

my throat makes for a great end to this workday. The sight of Kate in a tank top, looking casual, yet still stunning makes me smile. She affects me, there's no denying it.

She turns around slowly and finds me watching her. Her head tilts just ever so slightly to the side. "You're staring at me," she says quietly.

"Not staring. Watching." I don't try to hide that I'm watching her...that she turns me on.

She nods slowly, and her eyes drop to the beer in my hand. "Care to join me on the patio? I'd love to hear more about what brought you to Los Angeles."

I inhale sharply, not really wanting to share why I'm here, but I also have no intention of saying no to Kate. She stands up and reaches for the glass of wine she left on the sofa table.

"Come on." She smiles and walks past me, our shoulders brushing as she moves to the French doors that open to the back patio. I follow her outside and she sits down in an oversized patio chair with thick cushions and big pillows. I take the seat next to her while she curls her feet up under her long legs and spins her wine glass in her hand.

"I swear, this patio is my favorite part of this house," she says, tipping her head back and looking up into the sky. Small landscape lights shine on the shrubs and trees lining the perimeter of the yard, but it's not enough light to detract from the bright stars.

"I can see why," I remark. "I had no idea the foothills are literally in your backyard."

She laughs. "It's a blessing and a curse. They're gorgeous, but we get lots of wildlife. Rabbits that eat my plants, and even the occasional coyote looking for food makes his way over the fence and into the backyard. And I've yet to see one, but my neighbor told me he had a snake." Her eyes grow wide with fear at the idea. "I'd die. I honest to God would die if there was a snake in my backyard." She visibly shudders when she says that. "So I pretend they don't exist."

I actually laugh out loud. "It's amazing what we can do when we imagine things don't exist," I respond, those words searing a fresh wound on the scar I thought had finally healed.

Her eyes study me for a moment. "So what brings you to Southern California, anyway?"

I hesitate before answering her because I'm not sure how much I want to tell her. She's a stranger, my landlord, and also my boss's sister. I keep my guard up, but answer her as honestly as possible. "Just needed a change. An opportunity presented itself, and I jumped on it."

"Why did you need a change?" She presses the rim of her wine glass to her lips, tipping it back ever so slightly for a drink. Her pink lips part as the liquid hits her tongue, and I shift in my seat. Her eyes study me closely as I observe her in return, her head tilting to the side as she waits for me to respond.

Swallowing hard, I look away, out across the expanse of the backyard, beyond the grass line to the rolling foothills that are pitch black under the dark sky.

"I sense I struck a nerve," she says cautiously.

I shake my head and turn back to her. "Nah. I've just never really talked about it with anyone other than the psychologist the department made me see."

Her eyes widen and she shifts uncomfortably in her seat. I run my hand over my face and sigh loudly. Maybe it'll do me good to tell this story to someone else. Only this 'someone else' I find myself strongly attracted to, and I'm not sure I want her to know the fucked up details of my life.

"Are you okay?" she asks apprehensively, her eyes full of concern.

"I think so," I answer honestly.

"You think so?"

I chuckle. "I'm fine, I promise. It's been a crazy year and a half."

She nods in response, picking up on my hesitation to say more. "You don't have to—" she starts, but I interrupt her. I don't want her to think I'm a sociopath or that she's in any danger.

"No. It's fine." I smile at her. "Just nerves."

She takes another sip of wine.

I take a long breath in and exhale loudly before I begin. "About a year and a half ago, I was in the middle of a huge investigation," I catch her setting her wine glass down out of the corner of my eye as I focus on the large Ficus tree way out at the end of the yard. "I'd been working on this case for years, trying to bring down a mid-sized cartel."

She listens quietly, her full attention on me.

"I ended up falling in love with the girlfriend of one of the main suspects—who also happens to be my biological brother."

I hear her inhale sharply, but she doesn't move a muscle waiting for me to continue. The memory stings, and as I continue I try to keep my voice steady and my emotions at bay.

"We took down the cartel, in the process killing my father and his right-hand man. My brother took a plea deal—and the girl," I add, trying not to sound bitter. "And I got shot up in my driveway and almost died. To say that I didn't expect it to go down quite like that would be an understatement."

"Jesus," she mumbles.

We sit quietly for a few moments before she asks softly, "Your brother…do you have a relationship with him?"

That's a good question. "I don't know how to answer that," I admit honestly.

She shifts in her chair again, gripping a pillow to her stomach. "I mean, how does one of you end up in a cartel and the other on the side of the law?"

"Now that's a long story," I chuckle. "The condensed version is my father's cartel is what ended up killing my mother. She was murdered when Alex and I were young. My dad took Alex and groomed him for the business. My aunt and uncle adopted me, and I was raised by them. On one hand, I was so jealous of Alex and my father's love for him, but on the other hand, I was truly the lucky one." There is so much more to this story, but I'm not ready to reveal every fucked up detail of my past.

She nods in agreement, shock written across her face.

"It was that anger that drove me into the ATF, and I made it my mission to bring down my father and his business."

"Tell me about….her," Kate says quietly.

I turn my head and look at her; her questions are personal, yet she's not pushy. She's inquisitive, and I can tell that the meaning behind them isn't malicious.

"She was a witness. I had my eye on her because she was the daughter of a judge that was involved in my father's case. Alex stumbled across her, and I assumed he knew who she was. I thought she was in danger, so I moved in." There's still a slight ache in my chest when I think about Emilia, although with each day the ache fades more and more. "In the process, I fell in love with her. Fast. She was young, naïve, and there was something so innocent about her. I was worried Alex was going to hurt her or pull her into his world—" My voice cuts out as emotions bubble to the surface.

"But he didn't?"

"Didn't pull her into his world?" I shake my head. "Not really. He was on his way out. But she was definitely in danger for a while."

"And they're still together?" Her eyes search mine, desperate for answers.

I press my beer bottle to my lips and pour the beer down my throat, letting the sting replace thoughts of Emilia. "Married with a daughter. Live on the coast in Oregon."

"Do you still love her?"

That question feels like a punch in the gut, not because of the question, but because I've never allowed myself to answer it. "I thought I did," I admit. "But the more I talked about her to my therapist, the more I believe I was in love with the idea of her. Someone innocent. Someone who needed me. Someone who I felt I could steal away from my brother." The idea of Emilia doesn't hurt me like it should when you love someone.

Kate's eyes narrow on me in confusion. "Soooo…"

"The answer is no," I fill in. "I don't think I ever loved her. I'm not going to lie and say it didn't hurt when she chose Alex over me, but I don't think I ever really loved her in the way you're supposed to love a person. I loved that I could 'win' her over, I loved that Alex might be hurt if she chose me."

She just sits quietly, not saying anything.

"Pretty fucked up, huh?" I chuckle darkly. "I promise I'm not some nut case that just rented your house."

She shakes her head and laughs. "I don't judge. It sounds to me like your therapy has helped you see what it is you need versus what you thought you wanted, and I'm so happy you've recovered from your injury and you're able to return to work. So many agents aren't as lucky as you." There's a spark of sadness in her eyes. A look that only the friends and family of those in law enforcement get when they think of those who aren't as fortunate as I am.

I nod in agreement. "Which is why I was excited to take this opportunity here in L.A. with your brother. He's giving me another chance to prove myself. California is a fresh start for me." I smile at her and she smiles in return, and it's soft, caring, and does things to me that I'm not sure I'm ready for.

"So what do you do?" I ask, turning the questions on her. I'm done spilling my garbage. I want to hear about her.

She drops her eyes from mine and takes another drink of wine before resting it on her thigh. "I'm an attorney. I do corporate law, mostly negotiating and reviewing contracts. It's extremely boring to someone who's not interested in legalese, but it keeps me busy and pays well." She shrugs.

"Do you ever end up in court?"

"No. Ironically, if there is ever litigation, we typically hire outside counsel. Sounds weird, doesn't it?" She scrunches her nose up and smiles.

"Not really." I shake my head. "I get why. You're an expert at what you do. The attorneys you hire are experts in litigation. Everyone does what they do best."

"Exactly."

Our conversation slows, but it's not uncomfortable in the silence. We both relax in the quiet and just 'be'. There's something to be said for that level of comfort when you're in the presence of someone else.

"So, when do you think you'll be moving in?" she asks.

"I'm having some stuff delivered this weekend, so I hope Saturday is okay?" I raise my eyebrow at her, hoping it's not an inconvenience.

She smiles. "Saturday is perfect."

"I'm still waiting on a truck from Phoenix, so that'll be sometime next week, but I'm ready to get out of that hotel. Speaking of that hotel, I really should get going. It's getting late, and I didn't mean to keep you up." I stand up and she follows suit. We both carry our empty glass and beer bottle to the kitchen, and Kate swipes something off the center island.

"This is the key for the house." She dangles the ring on her pointer finger. "You can have your alarm system installed anytime. If you need anything secured before then, I have a safe and an alarm on this house. You're welcome to keep anything in here."

"I appreciate that." The soft tips of her fingers brush against my palm as she places the key in my hand.

"See you Saturday," she says, her voice barely above a whisper.

"See you Saturday," I return. For the first time in a long time, I have something to look forward to.

FOUR

Kate

"Katie," Nick's voice booms through the Bluetooth speakers in my car.

"What's up?" I ask, curious. My brother rarely calls me, especially at seven-thirty in the morning.

"I just wanted to see if you were really okay with letting Sam rent your guesthouse. I feel like maybe I jumped the gun and should've let you two speak before I just brought him over." He sounds stressed, and my gut tells me this call has nothing to do with Sam and my guesthouse.

I laugh and merge into traffic as I head into the office. "It's fine. I'm actually really glad you suggested him. It sounds like we're both busy, professional, and it worked out perfectly—I'm actually happy with the situation. He's moving in this Saturday."

"Whew," I hear him say and breathe into the phone. "I was feeling guilty. I rarely see you and here I am pushing my newest coworker on you."

"It's all good." Tired of beating around the bush, I finally ask, "So why'd you really call?"

"How'd you know?" he asks quietly, and I hear him shuffling papers around.

"Because I know you better than you know yourself," I respond, "and I can hear the strain in your voice. What's up?"

There's a long pause before he begins. "Nicole is pregnant again," he says quietly, his voice strained. Nick and Nicole, my brother and his wife. College sweethearts. The couple everyone wants to be. Parents of two of the cutest little boys in the world are having another baby.

"What! That's great news!" I'm genuinely excited for him, but I could hear the trepidation in his voice. "Why are you not excited, Nick?"

"Is it bad that I'm not excited?" I feel like I can hear him cringe.

"Yes," I answer bluntly. "Look, I know you said you were done after Joey and Jack, but a third baby isn't the end of the world. The boys are going to kindergarten next year, and this'll give Nicole something to do for the next five years," I laugh.

He mumbles something under his breath, and then says, "She was going to go back to work. She's really having a tough time coming to terms with this, which is making me have a tough time, too," he admits honestly.

"Want me to come by after work tonight? Talk to her?"

"Would you?" I can hear the desperation in his voice.

"I'd love to. I'll try to be there by seven."

"You're the best, Katie."

"I know, Nicky," I say warmly.

"Don't call me that," he says flatly. I laugh out loud. I love my brother and love to give him a hard time. "Love you."

"Love you, too. See you tonight."

I'm late, as usual. Work got busy, contracts needed to be reviewed and sent to attorneys overseas before I left for the day, and I'm always an hour late, if not more for everything. I drive as fast as I can in Southern California traffic to get to Nick and Nicole's before the boys go to bed.

I barely make it there as both boys are freshly bathed and bundled in their pajamas, waiting for me at the door.

"JJ!" I yell as both little monkeys jump into my arms. "How are my favorite boys?" Joey clings to me, his arms practically strangling me. "Easy there." I tug on his arm.

"Mom says we can't stay up," Jack pouts.

"Well, your mom is right." I tap Jack's nose with the tip of my finger. "It's late, and you two need to sleep. You have a big day at preschool tomorrow."

"All we do is play," Joey says, sliding off my knee.

"Well, playing takes a lot of energy, and you get that energy from sleep."

They both moan at my response. I giggle and take each of them by the hand. We head toward the kitchen where I assume Nick and Nicole are because I smell delicious food coming from that direction. My stomach growls in response.

"There you are!" Nick says, scooping up one boy in each arm. "Say goodnight to your aunt Katie, boys."

"Niiiight," they both groan simultaneously.

Nick kisses my cheek and heads off down the hall toward the boys' bedroom with one boy draped over each of his shoulders. I love seeing him with the boys and can't wait to see him with a third baby. I watch Nick with admiration and a bit of sadness. He reminds me so much of our father right now. Losing my parents within a year of each other was the single hardest thing Nick and I have been through. My dad had cancer and he succumbed quickly, and a year later my mom had a massive heart attack. We think the stress of my father's passing ultimately took its toll on her.

"I'll bring ice cream next time," I holler, and both boys start squealing. I hear Nick mumble something under his breath before the sounds of their voices trail off further down the hall. When I turn around, Nicole is walking over to meet me with a glass of wine in her outstretched arm. Her eyes are pink, and I can see the exhaustion on her face.

"How are you feeling?" I ask, taking the glass of wine from her as she wraps her arms around me. Nicole is the sister I never had. I lucked out when Nick married her. She's kind and caring and an all-around amazing wife and mother.

"Miserable," she says against my chest. "I barfed all morning and have been nauseated all day."

"Ugh," I mutter, resting my chin on top of her head. She's petite and I feel like a giant next to her barely five foot frame.

"And opening that bottle of wine for you and Nick about damn near killed me. Do you know how bad I want a glass right now?"

I start laughing. I know I shouldn't, but I do.

"Bitch," she mutters jokingly, pulling away from me and heading back toward the kitchen.

I follow right behind her, sipping on the chilled wine. "Sorry I'm so late—" I start, but she puts up her hands to stop me. They're used to me never being on time.

She just shakes her head. "Dinner is almost ready." She opens the oven and pulls out a pan of roasted potatoes.

"You didn't have to make dinner," I answer, feeling guilty that she's cooking when she feels so terrible. I didn't come over to be fed, but I'm never one to turn down a home cooked meal. "But it smells amazing."

"Tri-tip, your brother's favorite." She glances over her

shoulder at me and smiles. Nicole really loves Nick and this makes me happy. To know that she'd go out of her way to make his favorite meal, even when he should be cooking for her, shows me how much she loves him.

"You're a good wife, Nic." I set my glass of wine on the kitchen island and slide onto a stool. I watch her sprinkle the potatoes with parsley before she puts them in a large ceramic serving bowl.

"Smells amazing!" Nick says as he joins us back in the kitchen.

"Boys go down okay?" Nicole asks as Nick takes over in the kitchen and scoots her toward the other stool next to me.

"Easy peasy," he says as he pulls a carving knife from a butcher block. "We read *Goodnight Moon*, said prayers, and out they went."

"You make it sound so easy," I snicker, and Nicole rolls her eyes. I can see her hesitation and worry about adding another baby to their family, but they're both amazing parents and I just know she'll settle into this soon.

"It is," Nick chides.

"Okay, enough kid talk!" Nicole holds up her hand to stop Nick from saying anything more. "I want to hear about this new roommate of yours." She smiles and glances over at Nick to see if he's listening. He doesn't budge, but I see his shoulders tense as he carves the tri-tip into slices. "Is he hot?"

"Jesus Christ, Nicole!" Nick barks, and we both burst out laughing. I nod quickly, and her eyes widen in surprise.

"He is." I try to contain my smile. "He's really nice, too."

"What does he look like?" Nicole rubs her hands together and scoots her stool closer to me.

I lean in and talk quietly. "He's tall and has this perfectly tan skin and brown hair. He obviously works out because he's basically a wall of muscle." She closes her eyes as I describe him. "The first time I saw him, he was wearing a dark gray suit with a white shirt. His suit hugged every damn muscle on his body. He's got short hair that's not too short. Like he styles it in the morning, but must run his hands through it at work, and by the end of the day it's kind of mussed up, but in a way that looks like it's supposed to be like that." I can feel myself smile as I describe him.

"That's because our jobs are fucking stressful," Nick chimes in.

Nicole and I both ignore him as I continue. "And he's got these really *huge* hands—"

"You know what they say about big hands, right?" Nicole jumps in. She's literally bouncing in her seat as I describe Sam.

"Enough!" Nick barks at us, and we both crack up. "And that's not true," he grumbles, turning around to shake the knife at us. He rolls his eyes, and we continue to giggle like little girls.

"Anyway, he was not at all what I was expecting."

"He sounds perfect."

"He is pretty perfect. Too bad he's my tenant." I sigh and pick up my wine glass, finishing what was left.

"Who says you can't screw your tenant?" Nicole asks, resting her elbow on the kitchen island.

"*I* say she can't screw her tenant," Nick says loudly, carrying the platter of cut up tri-tip over to the kitchen table with a disgruntled look on his face. "Plus, wouldn't it be weird, you know, to date the guy who works for your brother?"

"It would only be weird if you made it weird," Nicole answers, raising her eyebrows at him. "And you wouldn't do that, would you, Nick?"

He stands with his hands propped on his hips and looks between us, but I don't let him answer.

"You guys, no one is shagging anyone, and no one is dating anyone." I stand up and reach for the bottle of wine to refill my glass. "He's nice to look at," I continue, "and he'll pay his rent." I raise the bottle of wine in Nick's direction and he nods in approval, so I fill a glass for him before setting it down. "It's a win-win."

"Well, I want to meet him," Nicole says, sliding into her chair at the dinner table. "And if, in addition to his rent, you got a little side action..." She wags her eyebrows at me, and I stifle a laugh. "...no one would judge you."

"I'd judge her!" Nick slams his fork down on the table. "No one at this table is sleeping with Sam Cortez. Got it?" His head moves from side to side as he looks from Nicole to me and back to her. We both burst into laughter, and Nick visibly relaxes.

"Can we talk about something other than Sam?" he asks politely, rubbing the back of his neck.

"Why, yes." I wink at Nicole. "Let's talk about this baby you two are going to have."

Nick lets out a deep sigh and looks at Nicole. She offers him a tight smile, and I sit down at the table opposite her, with Nick on the end. "Why are you two stressing about this baby so much?"

Nicole reaches for Nick's hand, and he laces his fingers through hers, resting their hands on the table.

"I'm old," she says honestly. "By the time I have this baby, I'll be thirty-five. Do you know that's considered advanced maternal age? I have to have all kinds of other tests, and what happens if something is seriously wrong with the baby?" Her voice breaks with emotion.

"What if?" I ask, looking back and forth between the two of

them. "You both said when you were pregnant with the boys that you'd take whatever God handed you...good or bad. What's different about this baby?"

Nicole shrugs. "I guess I was hoping to go back to work next year. I've taken almost six years off. I've kept up my license, but I was ready to get back to my career." Her eyes fill with tears. "I want to feel like I'm contributing to something more than wiping butts and making dinner," she says candidly.

"Nic," my brother responds as tears fall from her eyes. "You keep this family together. I don't know what we'd do without you."

The room falls silent as Nicole is overcome with emotion and Nick tries to comfort her.

"You know, there's nothing wrong with daycare," I finally say. "You can go back to work full-time, or even part-time, and the baby will be just fine."

Nicole looks up at me and wipes her tears. "I guess we've never really talked about that before." She looks over to Nick. "With the boys, it didn't make sense because having two in daycare was more expensive than the paycheck I would've brought home."

"I know this is stressful," I begin. "But you know I'm a believer in everything happening for a reason. There is a reason for this baby." I smile encouragingly at Nicole, and she offers me a weak smile back as she wipes her nose on a napkin. "Let this news sink in. Talk about all the options you have, and don't rush into any decisions. I promise you this is going to be a good thing."

She nods quickly and looks over to Nick, who's watching her carefully. "Nic, whatever you decide...work or no work, you know I'll support you one hundred percent."

"I know you will." She leans in and presses a kiss to his lips.

He holds her face. "This is going to be good," he says softly, and she nods again.

"It is," she responds, trying to convince everyone, including herself.

"Can we eat?" I ask, breaking the mood. "I'm starving."

Nick and Nicole both chuckle and Nick winks at me, a giant smile on his face. That's his way of saying thank you, and I couldn't be more excited for my sweet family to get a little bit bigger.

FIVE

Sam

I spin the key to my new house around my forefinger, holding onto the memory of Kate's fingers grazing my palm—soft and gentle, but electric at the same time. I still see her long light brown hair falling in pieces around her shoulders, dancing across her delicate collarbones, and her full lips turning into the most beautiful smile I've ever seen.

I try to shake thoughts of her out of my mind, but the clock on the wall taunts me. Mere hours until I'll be living within feet of her. Inches from where I could touch her, kiss her—feel her.

My bags have been packed for days and now sit by the door as I wait to bust out of this hotel room. A delivery truck is scheduled to arrive at the new house between eight and ten o'clock this morning, which means it's time to check out and stop for a coffee on my way to my new home.

Fifteen minutes later, I'm on the freeway, a steaming coffee in my hand and the morning sun guiding my way. A new day, new home, new beginnings. I pull into the quiet neighborhood and park on the street in front of the house. I grab my large duffle bag from the backseat, leaving a few small boxes and suitcases in the trunk before heading toward the guesthouse. Following the stone walkway around the side of the main house, I head to my new front door.

There's a pot of flowers on the porch. Sitting amongst the flowers is a white envelope with my name scrawled on the front. I reach for it, clutching it in my fingers as I open the front door. Sunlight filters in through the skylights, reminding me how bright and beautiful this place is. I toss the envelope and key on the kitchen island and carry the duffle bag down the hall to the bedroom.

After setting the bag in the corner of my new room, my cell phone rings, alerting me to the arrival of my new bedroom furniture. Forty-five minutes later, I have an entirely new bedroom set up: bed, dresser, nightstand, and oversized chair for the corner. I'm admiring my new space when I hear a soft knock on my door.

I can see Kate through the small panels of glass in the top portion of the door. Her light brown hair is twisted on top of her head, her hands cradling a giant mug as she waits for me to answer.

But I watch her for just a brief moment, her head tilted to the sky and her eyes squinting against the morning sun. Her lips are slightly parted, and I can just make out the move of her tongue running against her upper teeth. Those lips, that tongue…the things I want her to do to me with both of them. *Shit.*

With a deep breath, I shake off the thoughts of her ravaging me and open the door. I'm greeted with a giant smile just as her light perfume wafts into the space. "Welcome home," she says, pulling her bottom lip between her teeth. "Thought maybe you'd want some coffee." She holds the ceramic mug out for me.

"Thank you. Come in." I step aside and let her into her own guesthouse. Her eyes take in the barren space, and she looks back at me. "Looks like you're all settled," she says dryly, and I bust up laughing. She laughs in return and wraps her sweater tighter around her.

"I'd offer to help you unpack, but it doesn't look like anything is here." She spins around and looks down the hallway.

"Yeah, most of my stuff will get here later this week. I just had new bedroom furniture delivered, so that's what I've got for now." I shrug and pull the mug of coffee toward my lips, letting the steam billow around my mouth and nose before taking a drink.

She rocks slowly back and forth, from her toes to her heels, and I can't help but notice how fucking sexy she can make a pair of torn jeans and Converse tennis shoes.

"Well, I'm going to get out of your way." She juts her thumb over her shoulder, pointing to the door. "You know where to find me if you need anything." Her lips pull into another sweet smile as she opens the door and steps over the threshold.

"Hey, Kate," I call to her, hoping I don't sound too eager. She turns around and looks at me. "Thanks for the coffee." I raise the mug. "And the note. I haven't opened it yet."

She smiles wider and bites her bottom lip. *Fuck, that lip...*

I clear my throat. "But I feel very welcome here. So thank you."

"I'm glad you're here," she says before turning and walking away. Her long legs make her look like she's floating across the brick pavers, and she throws herself into one of the oversized lounge chairs on her back patio. She pulls a pair of sunglasses off the small table, sliding them onto her face as she picks up her own mug of coffee.

I could get used to seeing her like this every day. She will be my demise. Someone I wasn't expecting but am growing to want in ways I didn't think were possible.

"Cortez!" Nick's voice bellows from the office next door.

I spin in my chair and jump up, heading over to his office. "Morning," I greet him as I enter his office. He motions to the chair across from his desk and I take a seat.

He's standing with his office phone pressed to his ear as he leans in and reads something on his computer screen. He tilts the phone away from his mouth and whispers, "Did you read this shit?" He points at the screen, turning it so I can take a look.

"What is it?" I lean in, trying to make out what he's reading.

He holds his finger up to silence me while he quietly finishes his conversation. When he's finished, he places the handset down and looks up at me. "Navarro ring a bell?"

My eyes widen and I sit up straighter. Nick mentioned him before, but I wasn't sure he was going to let me in on this case. It's big. The bureau in Phoenix has wanted Navarro for years.

"What about him?"

"Well," he leans back in his chair and laces his hands behind his head, "we thought he went away when you took down the Estradas." He looks at me cautiously. "He didn't. He's moving guns and drugs through Tijuana now instead of Sonoyta."

"Who's he moving them through?" I rake my hands over my face, feeling my stress level begin to rise. These fucking drug cartels wear on me.

"Castillo."

"Fuck."

He nods in agreement. "My thoughts exactly. We got a tip

that it might be happening, but we didn't follow up immediately. When Estrada died, we thought Navarro would close up shop. He's got millions. He's old. He's a small operation. There was really no reason for him to continue. An informant from Jalisco provided us a sworn statement," he points at the transcript on the screen, "with all the details of his new business venture."

I nod and lean forward, resting my elbows on my knees.

"You know what this means, Sam, right?"

My stomach flips, and I'm not sure if it's excitement or fear.

"This is all you. You have the background and the history on Navarro. This is your case. Bring this fucker down." He offers me a tight smile and a sincere look that tells me he trusts me. I swallow hard and nod again as my mind swirls with questions and plans.

"Cortez?" Nick pulls me from my thoughts. "You got this?"

I take a deep breath and look him in the eye. "I got this."

"Are you even supposed to be telling me this?" Alex asks softly. I can hear his daughter, my niece, laughing and playing in the background.

"No. But I need all the intel I can get on him. You know him better than anyone—"

"Used to know him," Alex cuts me off. "That was a long time ago, Sam."

My fingers grip my steering wheel and I weave slowly down the crowded Southern California freeway toward home. "It wasn't all that long ago, Alex."

"Well, it feels like a lifetime ago. And honestly, I want to leave that in my past."

"Just let me call you tomorrow. Pick your brain for an hour and we'll leave it at that."

I can hear his exaggerated sigh and then his silence. "Fine. I'll call you at eleven. Emilia is taking Gracie to a playdate or some shit like that."

I heave a sigh of relief. "Thank you, man. You have no idea how much I appreciate this."

"Well, you better never breathe a word of this to Em. We don't talk about the past, we don't live in the past, and this is definitely part of my past that I wanted to leave behind."

"I won't say a word, brother."

"We'll talk tomorrow then," he says quietly.

There's a click before the line goes dead and I drop my head back against the headrest. A million questions swirl through my brain, and memories of the case that almost killed me shadow my thoughts. My heart races as I think of the day I was pumped full of bullets. My eyes blur as I force back the memories I've tried so hard to forget.

I make a quick stop for a bottle of whiskey and Chinese takeout before finding myself on Kate's back patio, sipping my whiskey directly from the bottle while my Kung Pao shrimp gets cold in the takeout box.

"Wanna talk about it?" Her voice pulls me from my thoughts.

"About what?" I turn and find Kate standing just outside the patio door, a plastic bag hanging from her fingertips. She must've just gotten home, as she's wearing a tight black skirt that hits her just below the knees and a red blouse that's wrinkled around the bottom where she's pulled it out from her skirt.

She wiggles her bare toes on the patio and starts toward me.

"Well, you're drinking straight from a whiskey bottle and you haven't even touched what I assume is your dinner in that takeout box, so something must be up." Both of her eyebrows rise, and her lips purse as she nods toward my food.

I hold up the whiskey bottle and smirk. "I don't have glasses or ice, and that..." I nod back to the take out box. "Just haven't gotten to that yet."

She side-eyes the whiskey bottle in my hand, and I inwardly cringe that in just a few swallows a quarter of the bottle is gone.

"So do you want to talk about it?" she asks me again and sits down in the chair next to me, dropping the plastic bag from her hand onto the small side table next to her chair.

"Not really," I sigh, pulling the whiskey bottle back to my lips and pausing when I see her carefully watching me. Instead of taking a sip, I reach out and offer her the bottle.

She looks at the bottle and then back to me, twice. Finally, her long fingers reach for the glass bottle and she takes it, her eyes studying the amber liquid as it sways. She holds it in her hand carefully before lifting it to her mouth. Her pink lips part slightly as the rim of the bottle touches her bottom lip, and I wonder what those lips taste like. My body reacts as she tips the bottle back and takes a swallow of the amber liquid. I watch the muscles in her neck constrict as she swallows. The soft skin of her neck is calling to me, begging for my tongue, and the exposed skin of her chest that peeks out from her blouse is taunting me to drag my fingers across it. My body reacts, my pulse simmering as I watch her carefully. I fight back the need to taste and the desire to touch her until my balls begin to ache.

Her eyes close tightly as she downs more of the whiskey, the burn of the liquid all too familiar as I feel it still settling in my own stomach. When her blue eyes finally meet mine, she leans forward, her face mere inches from mine. Her eyes dance between mine, and her full lips twist into a grin. Lips I want to devour. Her tongue brushes her lower lip, teasing me, and the slightest hints of whiskey roll off her tongue when she begins speaking to me.

"Follow me," she says as she stands up, the whiskey bottle still wrapped tightly in her fingers. She grabs her bag off the table and saunters across the patio and into the open French door. I watch her tight ass sway from side to side with each step she takes, calling for me.

I let out a quiet laugh and grab my takeout box, following her inside. At the large island, Kate presses her hands to the edge of the granite counter, and her head drops forward. The bottle of whiskey and two glasses with ice are perched in front of her.

I stand across from her, mimicking her stance and wrapping my fingers tightly on the other side of the island. I lean in over the middle of the island, bringing my body close to her, and then I study her beautiful face, taking in every smooth curve and hard line. I notice a small mole just below her lower lip, and I instantly want to drag my tongue across it, across her full lips, down her neck, and over every inch of her body.

I reach down and pour a good amount of whiskey into each glass, pouring slightly more into mine. I round the end of the island, a glass in each hand and stand in front of Kate. Too close. So close I can smell her perfume and see the rise and fall of her breasts with each quick breath she takes. I've lost all rational thought when it comes to Kate, and my desire is going to get the better of me in mere seconds.

I lift my glass of whiskey and down it in a single swallow. The ice numbs the burn, and I smack my lips, enjoying the taste. Kate slowly reaches forward and takes her glass from my hand.

She swirls the amber liquid around the small chunks of ice before shooting the whiskey all in one swallow. She places her glass on the counter next to mine and turns back to me. I take two small steps, closing the distance between us. It's now or never. As I move in, there isn't a hint of hesitation on her face, and her blue eyes welcome me home.

SIX

Kate

It's impossible to deny the desire floating in the air around us; an entire conversation is happening between us without a single spoken word. One step and he's pressed against me, his lips crashing into mine, stealing my breath away.

Hungry yet gentle, his lips pull me into him.

"Sam," I muster between kisses.

He moves, trapping me between the island and his six-foot-two wall of muscle. His fingers twist into my hair as he kisses me, and then he suddenly stops, pulling his lips away slowly, breaking our connection. My head buzzes and I'm not sure if it's the whiskey or Sam, but it's a heavenly feeling.

"Kate," he breathes and rests his forehead against mine. "I'm sorry, I shouldn't have done that. I shouldn't have—"

"Stop," I tell him and hold his face between my hands. "Do it again."

He hesitates, closing his eyes for a moment, when I lean in and press my lips to his, my kiss an unspoken invitation. His fingers expertly work the buttons on my blouse, careful yet quick. His thumbs brush my collarbones as he slides the blouse off my shoulders, letting it fall to the floor.

He inhales sharply as he traces a line with his forefinger, down my chest and between my breasts, stopping on the front clasp. He looks to me for permission to continue. I take a deep breath and reach for his hand, pulling him closer to me. Lacing my fingers through his, I guide him out of the kitchen and down the hall to my bedroom.

I lead him into my room and fumble through the dark to turn on my small bedside lamp. It provides a dim light, just enough to see, but not enough that it's distracting. When I turn around, I find Sam sitting on the end of my chaise lounge, his elbows propped on his knees as he carefully watches me. I walk back to him and stand in front of him, looking down into his stunning brown eyes.

"You sure?" he asks, his eyes full of lust as he runs a hand up my outer thigh, brushing the sensitive skin just under the hem of my skirt. I take a step back and his hand falls from my leg to his lap. I reach behind me, lowering the zipper on the back of my skirt, and I shimmy out of it slowly. It falls in a pile around my feet, and I step out of it, kicking it aside.

An audible gasp escapes him as I stand before him in black lace panties and a matching bra. I thank myself for wearing my nice lingerie today and not my cotton panties that I've learned to love. I rock gently from foot to foot, my hips swaying along with me. Sam's eyes sparkle, and a small grin tugs at his lips. He reaches for me to come closer, but I stay back, keeping my distance. I see the hunger growing in his eyes and in his pants, and I try to contain the smile on my face, but I can't because I want him…all of him.

I unclasp my bra in the front and slowly slide the straps down each shoulder, gathering the lacy material in my hand and tossing it on the floor next to my skirt. My full breasts are on display, my nipples are tight as the cool air and the excitement of Sam's arousal hits me. I step toward Sam, who wastes no time in pulling me closer to him. He presses his lips against my stomach, lightly kissing me across my belly.

His fingertips brush the edge of my panties, and he lets out a small groan, which causes me to clench my thighs in anticipation. His fingers pull at the delicate fabric as he edges them down my hips, pausing momentarily before sliding them all the way down my legs. I step out of them carefully, while Sam examines every inch of me with his lust filled eyes. He licks his bottom lip as his fingers trace the soft lines my panties left behind on my hips. His fingers move softly across my skin before he moves them toward my center.

"Come here," he says, standing up. He guides me to the edge of my king-sized bed and eases me down. "Lay back," he orders me gently, and I slowly lower myself onto my back. My legs dangle over the edge until he lifts them. "Scoot back," he says, and I slide myself to the middle of the bed. My legs are spread wide, all of me is bare, exposed to him, and I'm feeling vulnerable and nervous, but there's something about Sam that makes me feel safe.

Sam stands over me, every muscle in his body flexing against his clothes as he watches me carefully. His head tilts to the left, taking in the sight of me, stark naked and sprawled out before him.

"God, you're fucking beautiful," he breathes. He unfastens his belt before unbuttoning his pants and letting them fall to the floor. His deft fingers make quick work of unbuttoning his shirt, but he pauses momentarily, shutting off the bedside light. I can hear him finally removing his dress shirt, and I can see the outline of his body from the moonlight peeking in through the window. A shiver runs through my body in anticipation of Sam's touch.

We're both quiet and exposed, shadows dancing around the room as Sam's figure moves, positioning himself between my legs at the end of the bed.

Both of his hands rub the tops of my thighs, starting just above the knee as they work their way up my legs. My hips begin to quiver, every nerve on high-alert as his fingers trail across my skin. My center aches for his touch, and my hips buck gently as his thumbs tease my inner thighs. No man has ever had me in knots like this before.

"I'm going to touch you, Kate. If you don't want this, you need to tell me now," he says in a husky voice as he leans in and presses his lips to my inner thigh.

I shake my head, begging him not to stop and anxiously awaiting his next move. My entire body shudders when he drags his tongue across the sensitive skin just as he rubs a finger across my center, parting me. His fingers are gentle yet hungry as he explores me. A moan escapes me just as his thumb rubs small circles and adds the perfect amount of pressure on my clitoris, sending my body into a perfect haze of pleasure.

"Sam," I muster as he brings me closer, and my hips gently rock in tune with the strokes his fingers make as he glides in and out of me.

"Baby, this is just the beginning." He gently removes his fingers from me and spreads my knees wider, pressing them into the bed. "I promise that I'm going to taste every inch of this perfect body—another time, Kate. But right now, I need to be inside you."

There isn't a muscle in my body that isn't trembling. Trembling in pleasure and anticipation. I inhale sharply at the feel of his cock pressing against my opening. With a gentle nudge, he begins to fill me. My body shakes as it adjusts to his welcome intrusion, and then I grip the comforter as he pushes himself entirely in. He groans as he completely fills me, while both of his hands tightly grip my inner thighs.

He takes his time at first, building up his pace. My hands find his on my thighs, and he laces his fingers through mine as he continues to move in and out. My body is conflicted, a mix of pleasure and pain as I take all of him in.

"Kate," he hisses as his breathing hitches, and his speed quickens. His head tips back, and he squeezes my fingers and thighs tighter as he steadies his pace. Unwinding his hand from mine, he begins working my clit again. My back arches, and every nerve in my body begins to tingle. He immediately notices the change in my body. Picking up his pace again, he withdraws and slams into me. That battle between soft and caring and hard and rough is waging a war on my body, a war I know I'll succumb to—which one will be the victor is yet to be seen.

As my body spirals into ecstasy, I feel Sam's release. Our bodies are a mess of tangled legs and sweaty skin. Sam lowers himself on top of me, chest to chest. My body is numb from pleasure. Nothing but the labored sounds of both of us trying to catch our breath fills the space around us.

"See what you do to me?" he whispers against my ear. "I'm not even close to being done with you." He presses a gentle kiss to my cheek and pulls me closer. His hand rests on my chest, his finger drawing circles across my collarbone.

"Hope you didn't have plans of falling asleep early tonight," he says, and I can actually hear the smile in his voice.

"I had no expectations for tonight," I tell him as I roll to my side and face him. I let my hands cautiously explore the hard lines of his stomach, up his chest, and finally resting against his cheek. "But this," I pause as I search for the words, "this far exceeded anything I thought would happen."

"Is that the whiskey talking?" he says with a deep laugh.

"No," I answer honestly, and I feel his body tense for a moment before relaxing.

He pulls me closer yet again and quietly whispers, "Good."

SEVEN

Kate

I'm not sure what time we finally fell asleep, but when I come to I hear the light sounds of Sam's breathing next to me and I slide over to him. His warm skin presses against my cool skin, causing goose bumps to form along my arms. Even when he's asleep, I can feel the electricity between us. The chemistry is undeniable. I reach out and rest my hand on his firm chest, dragging the pads of my fingers across his hard pectoral muscle. It's there that I feel the firm ridges, the bumps of flesh that are not flush with the rest of his skin. My fingers tremble as I touch the scarring. As if he knows I've found his secret, his steady breathing suddenly stops, and I feel his entire body jerk, causing me to stop my exploration.

"I should go," he says quietly, his voice hoarse as he tries to shrug off my touch.

I won't let him run. I wrap my arm around his chest, holding him tightly. "Talk to me," I urge him, worried about the change in his demeanor. He told me how he was shot, he told me he was starting over—but something inside me tells me he's running, and I don't know if it's from the incident…or *her*. "Do you still love her?" I ask, even though I know I have no right.

I can feel his heart beating wildly against my arm that is keeping him trapped. Part of me feels guilty for holding him here, and part of me understands the need he has to protect his story. I'm as conflicted as he is. It's his story to tell in his own time.

I carefully withdraw my arm, releasing my hold on him, an invitation for him to leave. I can barely make out the rise and fall of his chest in the pre-dawn hours, yet I feel like I can see inside his soul. He's hurting and he's going to push himself away from me.

He carefully sits up on the edge of my bed, his back to me as I retreat to my side of the bed. He must sense me distancing myself because he looks over his shoulder as I pull the sheet up over my naked body in an effort to hide my embarrassment for being so pushy, but also to protect myself from what I expect will be his parting words…that what happened last night was a mistake.

"I'm sorry," I say so quietly I'm not even sure he heard me.

"Don't be," he responds, his voice almost as low as mine. He pushes up from the bed and stands naked before me, his perfectly toned backside just visible in the dusky room. "It's just not something I want to talk about. Please just let it go."

"Let what go? Talking about how you were injured…or her?"

He sighs as he bends down and steps into his boxer briefs before finding his pants and shirt. He carefully finishes dressing while I silently watch every move. My heart is racing as he prepares to leave, and I have no idea what he's thinking. He stands for a moment, looking at me, and I feel my lip begin to quiver. Why, I'm not sure. Then he drops his head and lets out another long sigh before heading to the door. He pauses just inside the doorway, turning around for a brief second.

"Please don't go." I ask him, my voice breaking. "I'm sorry for pressing you—"

"Thank you for last night, Kate," he says softly before leaving.

I close my eyes and feel my heart sink. I'm angry with myself for letting this progress to sleeping with each other, and I'm hurt that it will likely be a one-time thing when, for the first time in a long time, I want more. Tears slip from the corners of my eyes as I roll over onto my side and bury my face in the pillow he slept on. I can still smell the spicy hints of his cologne as I cry myself to sleep.

I would normally have left my house thirty minutes ago in an effort to beat some of the horrific Los Angeles morning traffic. However, this morning, I have no energy to get my ass into the office. My mind is distracted, full of thoughts, and my heart is heavy, full of emotions.

I lean against the kitchen island and look at the remnants of last night strewn across the granite counter. Shot glasses sit next to the bottle of whiskey, and two boxes of uneaten food sit untouched, reminding me of what led up to Sam being in my bed.

I drop a coffee pod in the instant coffee machine and push brew, staring at the thick brown liquid filling my coffee mug. Shoulders slumped, I transfer the coffee to my travel mug, grab my computer bag, and reluctantly head out the door. I'm not in the mood for work today, but I plan to bury myself in work, hoping it acts as a distraction to my wandering thoughts about Sam.

Settling into my car, I notice Sam's car is still parked up the long drive. I take a deep breath, wondering what he's doing and what he's thinking. Shoving those thoughts aside, I take a sip of coffee and drive away.

As I all but crawl through this shitty Los Angeles traffic, I hit Kandi's name on my phone and let the Bluetooth speakers in my car project the ringing of her phone.

"Hey," she answers, her voice strained.

"You okay?" I ask as I hear her shuffling around in the background.

She snorts and lets out a sad laugh. "I'm fucking exhausted," she replies. "Peyton was throwing up at three o'clock in the morning, and I've had Elena basically attached to my tit since four. Try caring for two kids, with one permanently attached to your boob, it's awesome," she musters, sounding like she's ready to snap.

"Need me to come over after work?" I ask before taking another drink of coffee.

"I wish you could, but Josh will be home early tonight and I plan to take a bath—alone—and go to bed at six."

I laugh, though I feel sorry for Kandi. "I don't know how you do it." In a sense, I'm envious of Kandi's life. She has a husband who adores her and a two kids—things I didn't believe I wanted until I saw what I was missing.

She sighs. "Why are you calling? Is everything okay? You never call this early." Her voice is quick, and she sounds short of breath. I imagine her running around topless, with Elena still suckling on her breast while she's chasing Peyton.

"I'm fine. Just miss you," I answer.

"I miss you, too. How about dinner this weekend? Josh

needs to bond with these two more and I need to get drunk. I plan to pump and dump!"

I stifle a laugh. "Deal. I'll call you later this week to set up a day and time."

"Sounds good. I can't wait to see you, Kate."

"Can't wait to see you, too." I disconnect and start thinking about where we can grab dinner and drinks. I miss Kandi. She's one of my only friends outside of the office. She's reasonable and rational and will probably kick my ass into next week when I tell her I slept with Sam, but I need a healthy dose of Kandi's perspective to get me past this funk.

After parking, I rush into the office. Normally, I'm one of the first ones here. Today, the office is abuzz with activity, activity I normally ignore from the peace and quiet of my office. As I saunter casually through the office, trying to go unnoticed, I see Adam's office door wide open, with him perched on the edge of his desk, his eyes following me all the way to my office. I try to avert his gaze as I feel like he can see right through my exterior, knowing what I did last night.

I close my office door behind me and toss my computer bag on my desk. Three rapid knocks on my door startle me, but before I have a chance to even answer, Adam bursts in and closes the door behind him.

"Katie, Katie, Katie," he says with a smirk, leaning up against the door.

"What, Adam? Traffic was terrible. I have to get logged in." I reach for my laptop, pulling it from my bag before docking it and starting it up.

Adam shuffles across my small office and places both of his hands on the end of my desk. He leans in and narrows his eyes at me. "Traffic wasn't any different this morning than it was yesterday, or last Friday, or last Tuesday. You're never late because of traffic...and you have this," he points his finger at me and moves it up and down from my head to my feet, "look about you."

I blow a puff of air through my teeth and roll my eyes at him. "A look about me? It's called running late, and I have a lot of shit to do. Quit hallucinating and go back to work."

"Right there." He points in my face and smirks. "You do that thing when you lie, where you scrunch your nose a little bit and roll your eyes."

"Shut up," I swat his hand away, and he laughs.

"Seriously though, Kate. You've been leaving early, coming in late...does this have anything to do with that man you're renting your guesthouse to?" He raises his eyebrows as he waits for me to respond.

I try to act cool, but my back stiffens. "No," I lie and begin sorting through a stack of contracts sitting in the middle of my desk.

"You suck at lying, Katie." His lips twist into a disbelieving grin.

"You suck at thinking you know things that aren't really *things*," I snap at him.

He tosses his head back and laughs at me...because he's right. I suck at lying, and he can see right through my bullshit. That's why he's my best friend. "Tell me about him," he says, taking a seat in the chair across the other side of my desk. He starts rolling his fingers on the hardwood desktop as he waits for me to speak.

"Tell you what?" I sigh in defeat. Adam knows precisely how to break me down.

He smiles that sincere smile that tells me he's genuinely interested in what I have to say. That smile that tells me I can share anything with him and he won't judge me. That smile that tells me how lucky I am to have him as my friend. "Tell me why this guy, of all the guys you've met, dated, communicated with, shared a drink with...what about this one has you so out of sorts? It's not like you to be like this, Katie."

I rub my temples and look at Adam. With a little shake of my head, I answer him honestly. "I don't know." I glance distractedly over at the large watercolor painting in my office. "There's just something different about him."

"Different, how?" he questions, raising his eyebrows.

I shake my head again and look Adam directly in the eyes. "I don't know."

"Huh," he says, leaning back in his chair. "I want to meet him." Adam always does this. He's protective in this brotherly kind of way, which I appreciate, but at times can also be overbearing...like right now.

"I appreciate what you're trying to do," I start. "But as quickly as I thought things had started, I'm afraid they may have fizzled out just as fast." I try to control the emotion in my voice, but he just looks at me, his brows furrowed and his jaw tense.

"You slept with him, didn't you?" His eyes narrow slightly.

"Adam, don't ask me that question." I can feel my cheeks instantly blush.

"Why, because you did, or because you don't want to lie to me?" He knows he's pinned me into a corner.

"Both," I answer, and he exhales loudly.

"Katie," he says, with a *tsk* after my name. "We've talked about this—"

"I know," I tell him, holding up a hand to shut him up. "I know we have. And you know what, I threw caution to the wind. I let my guard down and let Sam in."

"You bet you did," he mumbles, and I choose to ignore his snide remark as he rubs his chin.

"I have to live with what I've done and also live with the fact that he's my tenant!" My voice is rising, and Adam's eyes grow wide.

"Shit, Katie," he huffs, his eyes full of sympathy.

"I know," I groan. "This is so bad." I rest my elbows on the edge of my desk and rub my eyes.

"It's going to be fine. So you slept with the guy that you're renting to." He snorts but collects himself quickly. "Think of it as a one-night stand. You got what you needed and now you're moving on."

I exhale loudly, and he looks at me. "You're not moving on, are you?" he asks with an exaggerated sigh.

"How?" I plead. "I really like him."

Adam shakes his head at me. "You just have to. It's what's best for your situation. You can't continue to sleep with your tenant, Katie. That's weird."

I stare at Adam across my desk and fight the urge to bury my face in my hands and cry. I'm feeling emotional because I want more with Sam. Everything about him intrigues me, and yet I barely know him.

"What do I say to him?" I ask, hoping Adam has the answers. That he'll just magically know what I should say, and all of this will be behind me, except I know that's a lie. Because my heart won't get over Sam that quickly. Something about him has pulled me to him.

"How do I approach him?"

He looks at me sympathetically. "You just need to talk to him as soon as possible. Tell him it was a mistake and you're sorry."

"It wasn't a mistake," I mutter.

"Yes, it was." He leans forward, capturing my hands and pulling them into his. "We all make mistakes. You'll get over this, just like you got over all the other ones, I promise." He smiles at me. "And you'll find a great guy. One you're not renting your house to. I know you will." He gives my hands a tight squeeze.

I offer him my best fake smile, and he winks at me. I don't know what I'd do without Adam.

Without another word, he pushes himself up and walks toward the door, only to stop and turn toward me. "You've got this." His lips pull into a tight smile. After he leaves, I finally bury my face in my hands and have a good cry.

EIGHT

The ringing of the phone sounds through the speakerphone on my desk, and I spin a pen between my fingers while I wait for Alex to answer.

"Sam," he answers after the second ring. Alex and I are still working on our relationship, and I'd be lying if I said I still didn't get a bit of anxiety when I talk to him. The years of separation, lies, and living on opposite sides of the law seem to have created a certain level of distrust between the two of us.

"Hey, Alex," I answer him. "Thanks for taking my call."

"Yeah, no problem."

"Is now still a decent time to talk?" I doodle on the legal pad in front of me, trying to tamp down my anxiety.

"Yeah, but I've only got a few minutes—"

I cut him off. "Then let me jump right in. I need to know everything you know about Navarro."

He inhales sharply, and then clears his throat. "You don't ask for much, do you?" He half laughs but continues. "He's a smart guy and runs a tight ship. A very shrewd businessman. His circle is tight, and he doesn't make mistakes." I hear the warning in what he's telling me. It's going to be tough to get any information on his organization.

"Did you deal much with him?" I always wonder, now that Alex is out of the business, if he'd be fully honest with me. I have to trust that all the information he provides me is enough that I won't be in danger, but there is always a little apprehension on my part.

"Not much. When we were crumbling, he offered his services, but Dad never wanted us depending on another organization...because when you owe favors, you get pulled into shit, and when you get pulled into shit, you lose control. He never wanted to lose control."

If that isn't the damn truth. It took us years to get enough intelligence to finally bring charges against my father. Once we did, it was the beginning of the end of his business. In a matter of months, all the men that were working for him were either locked up or dead—all except for Alex. My brother. The other half of me.

"Understood," I answer him. "Any idea what he's moving?" I tap my pen on the notepad, ready to document every detail Alex can provide.

"The usual—guns, weed, cocaine, heroin."

"Any idea where the guns are coming from?" I know the answer, but I'm curious to see what Alex knows.

"Not confirmed, but through Colombia via Russia." That's exactly where they're coming from. "I used to know all the details for all of our competitors, but it's been a while, and honestly, I'm trying to forget."

"I know, and I appreciate you telling me what you do know." I mean that. I know how hard it is to get out of that life. The last thing he needs is me knocking on his door, asking for information, but right now I want every last detail on Navarro.

"That's all I really remember—Oh, one more thing. Girls," Alex says, his voice hitching.

"Girls?" I question. "He moves girls?"

"Not exactly. He has a weakness for them. He owns strip clubs, does most of his business exclusively in these clubs."

That I knew, but I didn't know he owned them. Another front for moving money. I note that.

"And he always has a handful of girls servicing him. Trust none of them. But if you can get someone inside, that might be your ticket to getting everything you need."

"Shit," I utter into the phone. Alex just handed me the fucking jackpot. "I can't thank you enough," I tell him as I furiously scribble notes.

"And be careful," he says, his tone serious. "He's dangerous, and he won't go down without a fight."

I'm touched by Alex's concern for my safety. "I understand. If you think of anything else, I'd really appreciate it."

"Yeah, of course," he says. Silence overtakes the phone line, and I'm about to end the call when Alex begins to speak again. "So, how are *you*?"

"I'm hanging in there." It's an honest reply. "Just adjusting to life in Southern California."

"How is it?" he asks, and suddenly the mood shifts. He sounds genuinely interested in what's happening in my life, and I'm caught off guard, in a good way. I never believed Alex and I would have a normal brother-to-brother relationship.

"I think I'm really going to like it here. The traffic sucks, but aside from that, I think it's exactly the change I needed."

He replies genuinely, "Good. I'm really glad things are going well for you."

"Thanks," I respond.

"And if I think of anything else about Navarro, I'll be sure to let you know."

"I really appreciate it."

"And, Sam," he adds.

"Yeah."

"Please keep in touch. You know, with things that don't have to do with your job." His voice is sincere, and some of the residual anger I've been harboring around Alex suddenly evaporates. A small sense of hope fills the void, and I pray that we will get to a good place.

I let out a small laugh. "Yeah, I can do that."

"Good. Be safe, brother." And the line goes dead.

It's the first time in a long time that I'm able to hang up the phone with him and not feel anger or resentment. The first time I genuinely enjoyed the briefest of conversations with him. The first time I didn't feel a hint of jealously over him and Emilia— and that's because all I can think about is Kate.

I'm a dick. The way I left things this morning weighs heavily on my mind. I've been staring at my cell phone all day, debating whether or not to call Kate…or send her a text apologizing for being the master dick that I am. Seriously, the fact that I'm even considering a text makes me a bigger dick.

I rub my head and decide to call it a night. Time to go fix shit and apologize for being the world's biggest dick.

I glance at my watch for what seems like the eighty-seventh time since I've been home. Through the large window, I watch

Kate's house, waiting for a light, for any sign that she's home. It's almost eleven o'clock, and my stomach is beginning to twist with worry.

I spin my cell phone in my hand as I contemplate calling her just to make sure she's okay. Just as I glance down at my watch again, the kitchen light in her house flicks on, and my heart suddenly calms. She's home.

Just as quickly as the lights turns on, though, they shut off again, and my stomach drops as I envision what Kate is thinking...what she's feeling right now. I finally press the call button on my phone, and Kate's name lights up on my screen. One ring. Two rings. Three...then four. No answer. Her sweet voice comes on the line, telling me to leave a message, but I hang up and press the call button again. After three rings, I finally hear her voice.

"Hello?" she answers softly, her voice raspy.

"Kate, I'm sorry to call so late," I start, and then pause for a moment. "I really need to talk to you." Silence fills the other end of the line, and I hear a light sigh before she begins.

"I'm really tired tonight—"

"Please," I cut her off. "Two minutes."

"Okay. Two minutes. I'll unlock the back door."

A sense of relief washes over me as the line goes dead. It takes me seconds to jog across the stone walkway and up to her back door. I hear the lock disengage just as I approach. The door opens slowly as I'm raising my hand to knock.

Kate steps aside, opening the door wider. I step inside, and without a second thought, pull her to me. She gasps as my lips hit hers. A million apologies are felt but go unspoken as I kiss her. She's hesitant, I can feel it, and she has every right to be.

"Kate, I'm so sorry," I whisper against her soft lips. I drop my forehead to hers and drink in the light floral scent of her perfume.

Her long hair is piled on top of her head, and she's changed into a pair of pajama shorts and a tight tank top. Every curve is on full display, and as much as I want to reach out and trace each one, I can't. I feel her body tremble under my touch, her shoulders slack and head dropped forward.

"You don't have to apologize," she says quietly. "It was a mistake. What happened last night should've never happened—"

"What do you mean, a mistake?" I ask abruptly, standing back a little and lifting her chin so she's forced to look at me.

Her eyes are glossy and red, and there's not an ounce of makeup on her beautiful face. Her cheeks are splotchy, and her nose is pink. She's been crying, and my heart breaks a little because I was the cause.

"Last night wasn't a mistake," I tell her. "What was a mistake is how I left this morning. What was a mistake is how I avoided questions that you had every right to ask me."

She shakes her head, and I hold her shoulders. "Yes," I stop her. "Kate." I hold both sides of her face and tilt her head back so she can't look away from me. "Last night was not a mistake. Last night is going to happen again, and next time I'm not going to leave."

Kate pulls out of my grip. "Sam," she says, backing away from me. Her eyes are full of hesitation. "We shouldn't—"

"We should," I sigh in frustration and pause. "I owe you answers, and I owe you an apology."

Her eyes turn glossy, but she takes a deep breath and steadies her emotions.

"I wasn't lying when I told you I don't love her," I tell her, shifting uncomfortably. "I'll always care about her, Kate. She's a part of my family now. She's married to my brother and the mother of my niece. I love her in a way that you love a family member, but I don't *love* her." Saying those words finally sets something inside me free. I feel like the weight of the world has been lifted off my shoulders, and my heart begins to opens. I don't love Emilia. I repeat it to myself and let those words settle in.

NINE

Kate

"But you did love her?" I question Sam, trying to understand how deep he was into this relationship with Emilia because this is a new one for me. The man I want to be with has an ex who's married to his brother. I almost laugh at the absurdity of it.

Sam rakes his hands over his face before running them through his hair. It's then I notice the dark circles under his eyes and the twelve o'clock shadow along his jawline. He looks about as terrible as I feel.

"It's complicated," he finally answers.

I back away. Because in my mind, it's not that complicated. Love is a yes or no answer. There is no in-between. There is no "kind-ofs" with love. You either love someone or you don't.

"Bullshit," I spit out.

"Kate—"

"Love can be complicated, Sam. But whether you love or loved someone is not! You either loved her or you didn't."

His jaw clenches, and I can see the rigid muscles flex and relax. "I thought I did," he says, stepping toward me again, closing the distance. "It's like I mentioned before, I was more infatuated with the thought of her—the girl my brother wanted. The brother I hated had her, and I wanted her." He outwardly cringes when he says that.

I let that sink in for a second. "You only wanted her because your brother had her?"

He tips his head back, squares his shoulders, and looks at me straight in the eyes. "In the beginning, yes. I did develop feelings for her...but I was never *in love* with her, Kate."

I drop my eyes and try to steady the rapid beating of my heart before he starts speaking again and I look back at him. "When I kissed her...it didn't feel like it does when I kiss you," he says, lowering his eyes to my lips. "She didn't feel like you feel in my arms. She didn't react to my touch like you do. She's not *you*, Kate." His voice hinges on desperation when he says 'you', and I waver with his admission.

"You don't even know me." I put my hand up to keep him from coming any closer, fighting his pull.

His eyes are full of hunger and want, and as much as I'm fighting against him, I'm falling for him twice as hard. "I don't know a lot about you, Kate—but I'd like to find out more." He captures my hand in his. "I'd like to know everything about you, Kate," he utters, bringing his lips so close to mine I can almost feel them.

I close my eyes and listen to the sound of my blood rushing through my ears and the pounding of my heart against my chest. Everything about Sam sets my body on fire.

"I'm sorry I didn't answer your questions this morning," he whispers against my face. "I was feeling vulnerable...and I hate feeling that way." I want to lean forward and capture his lips with mine, but instead I rest my forehead against his. Taking in his closeness and the scent of his fading cologne. "And this morning was the first time anyone has touched my scars," he admits quietly. Opening my eyes, pain is stretched across Sam's beautiful face.

"I'm sorry I touched you," I tell him and close my eyes again. I can feel him shake his head. He's now captured both of my hands in his, and we stand quietly in the middle of my kitchen, two people searching for answers that the other holds.

"Come here," he whispers, pulling me behind him. He opens the French doors and steps out onto the patio. I follow closely, and he closes the door behind us. We walk across the patio down to the walkway of his house, my bare feet padding along the stone path. He bursts through the door, pulling me with him, through the living room and into his bedroom. My mind is racing as he says nothing, only pulling me gently behind him.

Flicking on the lights, we walk through the bedroom to the bathroom and confusion sets in. "What are we doing?" I finally ask as we stand in front of the long bathroom vanity. Large light bulbs outline the oversized mirror. I had forgotten how bright this bathroom was with its stark white walls and light gray accents.

Sam's chest rises and falls as he looks at me, and then he closes his eyes for the briefest of moments before he lets go of my hand. In a single fluid motion, he pulls his t-shirt over his head and tosses it to the floor where it gathers in a bunch at our feet.

He stands before me, bare-chested, every single ridged muscle on full display. The curve of his shoulders is met by the swell of his bicep. Over his heart is a tattoo of a crest, an homage to his heritage I assume.

"Touch me," he says softly.

I tense. "Sam—"

"Please." His eyes beg me.

"Why're you doing this?" I plead, my hands shaking at my sides.

"Because I need you to touch me."

I stand here, lost in thought. His eyes close when he sees my hand rise, still shaking as I contemplate touching him.

"Do it," he begs, his eyes pinched closed.

His upper chest and shoulder are marred with scars, and my fingers tremble as I reach out to touch his golden brown skin. He inhales sharply when the pads of my fingers brush against the wide span of his chest, trailing down to his abdomen. His eyes remain closed as I reach another hesitant hand up and brush my fingers across his collarbone.

Sam's head falls forward slightly as my hands explore him. He startles me when his hand finds mine, stopping me. His strong hand wraps around mine, guiding me to the very place I was so hesitant to go.

"Touch me," he says again, and I do. His hand falls from mine as my fingers trail across the smooth raised scars, circling the soft flesh. I can feel his heart beating wildly in his chest.

Stopping, I lean in, and without thinking, press my lips to the large scar just below his collarbone. I press a gentle kiss to each raised scar, my lips connecting with his soft skin. Both of his arms engulf me, pulling me tightly to him. He has opened himself up to me, showing me the most vulnerable parts of him, and in this exact moment, I know I'm falling in love with Sam Cortez.

TEN

When Kate presses her lips to my scar, I lose control. My arms instinctively pull her to me. Embracing Kate, I let myself fall deeper for her. She's seen the ugly parts of me. My vulnerability, the urge to run, and my scars, yet here she is standing before me, showing me who she really is. She's honest and loving and not afraid of what I have to offer her. She's someone I don't deserve, yet selfishly, I want her.

"Kate," I say her name, my lips pressed against her soft hair.

"Hold me," she says in return, and my arms tighten around her. Something passes between us...an understanding, an apology.

"Can we start over?" I ask. She squeezes me in return and inhales deeply. Her head nodding against my bare chest gives me the answer I so desperately wanted. My thumbs knead the soft skin of her neck, and I can feel her relax in my arms. The angst that was present before has lifted.

Kate pulls herself from my grip and stands before me, her cheeks still flushed.

"I'm sorry for being so complicated," I tell her, and her eyes begin to mist over. She swallows hard, biting back her emotions. "I'm sorry that I brought my baggage to your doorstep...literally," I chuckle, and she fights back a small smile. "I promise to do better."

"Don't make promises you can't keep," she says quietly, and I can see the skepticism in her eyes.

"I promise to try."

"That's all I can ask," she says with a soft sigh.

I brush my knuckles against her delicate cheek, causing her eyes to close. Her pink lips are slightly parted and tempting me. Leaning in, I capture her mouth with mine. I apologize with my lips, and she accepts my apology in return with hers.

"Stay with me tonight, Kate," I mumble against her lips. She pulls back, cupping my face with her hands. "Let me hold you. Let me start over."

She blows a puff of air through her lips and leans in, pressing her forehead to mine. "As sincere as you just sounded, I doubt you'll just hold me." she breaks, letting a small laugh loose.

I love to hear her laugh, and I smile in return. "I mean, I'm not going to argue with you if want me to do more." I imagine her naked, sprawled across my bed, and my dick instantly hardens.

She wraps her arms around me and presses her face to my chest as she giggles. I guide her out of the bathroom to my bedroom where she sits down on the edge of the bed.

"Kate, I want you to stay, but please don't feel pressured to. I'm sure you're —"

She stands up quickly and walks over to me. "Shh," she begins, pressing her forefinger to my lips. I oblige as her intense blue eyes study mine. Her head tilts to the left, and she takes a deep breath, seeming to come to a decision in that moment. "I want to stay. I want to start over, Sam. But there won't be any sex tonight."

"I can accept that," I begin, although disappointed. "Just lay with me then. All I want is you next to me."

She offers me a sincere smile and nods once.

"Come here." I wrap her small hand in mine and pull her toward my bed, throwing the comforter back so she can climb in. Once she's settled in the middle of the bed, I climb in next to her and pull her against me.

She smells like the sweetest hints of coconut, and it takes every ounce of self- restraint to keep from pulling her on top of me. Her pajama bottoms and tank top do little to hide every curve on her perfect body. Her firm breasts press through the thin material of her tank, and I can feel the soft skin of her back peeking out from just above her bottoms.

"Sam?" My name rolls off her lips tenderly, and she pushes herself up slightly to look at me. "I'm going to need you to promise me something."

"Anything," I respond.

"I'm going to do something, and I need you to just go with it." She pulls her lips into her mouth and pushes herself up before she swings a long leg over my waist. She sits on top of me, her pajama shorts doing nothing to hide the heat from between her legs.

No sex, she said. Goddammit, all I want to do is rip her bottoms off and thrust into her. I close my eyes and breathe deeply, trying to not be affected by her warm center pressing against me, inviting me. The thin material of my shorts is doing nothing to hide my growing erection, and I know she can feel it because her lips have turned up into a sly little grin.

Kate shifts slowly, moving from side to side as she rubs herself against me.

"You don't play fair," I groan, gripping the sheets to keep myself from taking her.

She presses her palms to my lower abdomen where she lifts and lowers herself as she continues to move against me, the friction causing my dick to become rock hard.

Fuck her rules. I lift my hand and slide it down between us where I slip it under her pajama bottoms and instantly find her soft, wet flesh.

"Sam!" she warns and stops moving. I dip a finger inside her before obliging to her rules and pull my hand out. Her face tells me she wants more, but I let her take the lead.

She rocks her hips again before she slides further down my legs and pauses. Her palms move south with her, and in doing so her fingers catch the waistband of my shorts and boxer briefs. I lift for her, and she easily pulls them down my legs, discarding them at the foot of the bed.

My dick stands at attention, throbbing and hard as Kate moves to position herself over my thighs. She looks at me, that same sly smile twisted across her lips. She licks her lips just as she wraps her long fingers around my length. Her palm is warm and soft as she begins to stroke me gently.

I catch my breath, groaning in response. I hold on tightly to her thighs that are bent at my side, my fingertips gripping the silky flesh just above each of her knees. As she leans forward, her eyes fix on mine and she wets her lips. Her velvety pink lips part slowly as she leans in further and pulls me into her mouth.

"Jesus," I mutter as her tongue presses against the head of my dick.

She licks gently and slowly lowers her mouth further down my shaft. I can feel the back of her throat as her tongue rubs the underside of my dick in measured, sweeping strokes. She sucks lightly, tightening her grip on me before she begins dragging her lips up and down. I relish the feel of my cock in her sweet mouth. She's careful and attentive, and I'm so close to blowing that I have to gather my thoughts.

As Kate's lips suck and stroke me, I can see her hard nipples pressed against her silk tank. I reach over and pinch one, causing her to moan and look up at me. Her blue eyes shine with need as she works me, bringing me closer.

My dick hardens and my balls tighten as I'm about to come. I tap her arm to let her know my release is imminent, but she continues, taking me deeper. I can feel my release against the back of her throat as my entire body shakes with an orgasm. Kate slowly finishes, taking in every last drop of me. It's singlehandedly the sexiest fucking thing any woman has ever done.

She sits up, straddling me as she pulls her bottom lip into her mouth. Her hair is messy and falling out of the bun she had piled on top of her head. The straps of her silky tank top hang off of each shoulder, and the look on her face is priceless. She looks like she's just conquered the world, and she did. Mine.

ELEVEN

Kate

"You done?" He smirks as he pulls his arms behind his head.

"For now." There's an edge of snark in my tone. "Time to sleep." I begin to slide off of him, but he stops me.

"Clothes off," he orders with a giant smile. "We sleep naked in my bed."

"No sex, Sam," I remind him.

"No sex, Kate. Just sleeping." He winks at me. He pulls the covers back as I lift the hem of my satin tank and toss it to the floor. My breasts hang heavily, now on full display. A barely audible groan escapes Sam's lips as he reaches out and cups a breast.

I open my mouth to chastise him, but his grin widens. "You didn't say anything about touching." His lips pull my nipple into his mouth, and he sucks hard, causing my core to tingle. I can feel his dick beginning to twitch between us. I love that his body reacts this way to mine.

He moves to the other breast, his tongue circling and lips sucking. His fingers tug at the waistband of my pajama shorts, and I finally slide off of him so he can remove them. I fall back onto the mattress and he falls on top of me, settling between my legs. I can feel every inch of him hardening again, and I shake my head.

"No sex," I scold him, knowing damn well I can't say no to him.

"I heard you the first time," he growls, pressing a kiss to my breast. He's pushing the boundaries, and I'm letting him. No man has ever made me weak until him. "But you have no idea how bad I want to fuck you right now, Kate." He looks up at me, his eyes begging me to let him in. But I like having the control for now and I smile, pushing him off of me.

"I know." It'll happen again. Just not today.

"You're killing me," he mutters as he lies down on his side next to me. I can't help but let a small laugh loose as I sense his growing sexual frustration. "Fine. No sex," he grumbles, "but there won't be any sleeping anytime soon."

"Oh, yeah?" I question jokingly, just as his palm cups my core. I gasp at the connection and try to squeeze my thighs together, but I'm not quick enough. He has just enough time, and room, to slide a finger deep inside me.

"You're wet, Katie," he says huskily into my ear as he kisses the side of my face. It's the first time he's ever called me Katie, and I don't mind it when it rolls off his tongue. "I could feel you earlier...but now, you're even more wet." His lips brush my ear, sending shivers down my body.

"So..." I purse my lips to keep myself from smiling. This little game of push and pull is driving him wild.

"So...I'm going to take advantage of that." He uses his other hand to pull my knees apart, and I easily give in and let him. I succumb to Sam Cortez. I don't know that I'll ever be able to say no to this man. I become weak to his touch, and I'll give him anything he wants. The pad of his finger swirls around my clit, and my body instantly begins to tingle at his touch. His fingers are magic as they circle, slide, and push gently into me.

"You don't play fair, Sam." I'm barely able to muster as he works his fingers in and out and all around me. He leans forward, pulling one of my nipples between his teeth, and nibbles gently. Between my sensitive breasts and him working me close to an orgasm, my entire body begins to shake.

"You like that, huh, Katie." His voice is deep, raspy, and completely sets me on fire.

I can't speak, so I simply nod as my back arches and he brings me closer to the edge. Just as I'm about to fall, he pulls his hand away and my eyes shoot open. My breathing is rapid, my heart nearly beating out of my damn chest as fast as my impending orgasm begins to fade.

Sam sits up and licks his bottom lip. "What?" he asks, tilting his head.

I narrow my eyes at him. "You did that on purpose, didn't you?"

"Did what?" He grins.

"Brought me so close, yet not close enough."

He tips his head back and lets out a boisterous laugh. "Katie," he whispers as he leans in. "You don't get to control everything."

I roll my eyes at him and slide my hand down between my legs. "Who said?" I slowly begin to work myself, my fingers sliding in and out of my wet pussy. Of course, I'd prefer Sam's fingers, but I'm going to prove a point to him. Sam's eyes are heavy as he watches me, and he slowly strokes himself, matching my rhythm.

That familiar feeling is just beginning to arrive, that slight tingle telling me I'm not terribly far away from the brink of ecstasy. Only this time, my hand is suddenly pulled away and pinned above my head. His eyes are hungry and possessive as he maneuvers himself back into control. He sets a knee between my legs, and his hard erection bobs just at my core. With one lift of my hips, I could easily slide him inside me.

He shakes his head as his brown eyes take me in. "I love the way you look naked underneath me," he says with a grin. "But I'm going to love the way you look even more when I make you come, Katie." And with both of my hands pinned in his left, he reaches down between us with his right hand and begins touching me again.

My body is lost somewhere between coming down and on high alert from all the back and forth. It takes him less than a minute to bring me back to the brink, only this time my entire body convulses as I'm ready to lose control.

My thighs shake and my back arches when Sam pulls my nipple into his mouth again, this time biting harder. My orgasm is just about to peak when he stops again and lays himself down on top of me.

His face pressed to mine, chest to chest, pelvis to pelvis. He's lined up at my center and ready. My body is in complete chaos, and I finally break down.

"Fuck me," I tell him, totally surrendering to him.

He smiles and presses a soft kiss to my lips.

"Please," I beg.

"No can do, Katie. You said no sex." He kisses my lips again, still holding my hands tightly above my head.

"I lied," I desperately beg. I actually try to angle my hips so that he'll just slide into me, but he shifts. And when he does, he laughs.

"Katie, Katie, Katie...." he mocks me. "I never took you for a liar."

I roll my eyes at him again. "Please, Sam. I need you inside me."

His body stiffens, and he gazes into my eyes. "My rules this time?"

I nod my head frantically. "Touch me," I beg him. "Now."

His eyes are fierce as he pushes himself up, never releasing my hands. His fingers slide back between us where he instantly finds my clit and pinches it, bringing me back to life. "You're insatiable," he says as he slides two fingers inside me, pumping them softly, while his thumb works me. My entire body begins to shake again when he suddenly removes his hand and slides his cock inside me. One quick motion and I come unglued. My body quivers around him as he fucks me—fast, yet gentle. My entire body is numb and on a high as he slides in and out of me. Blood rushes through my ears, and I momentarily lose my vision as my entire world is consumed by Sam and what he's doing to my body.

He finally releases my hands, and they lazily flop to my sides as my body has expended all of its energy on the way down. I'm officially tapped out. My head falls to the side as Sam groans and finds his own release inside me. He lowers himself on top of me, and I manage to wrap my arms around him.

He stays inside me, brushing the stray hairs off of my face. "How are you feeling?" he asks, pressing a kiss to the corner of my mouth.

"Can't talk," I barely muster as I'm still trying to catch my breath. "Amazing," I finally answer him.

"Don't tease me, Katie. I'll always win." He chuckles and slides out of me. I don't even have the energy to argue with him, but I'll get him back for this. "Now we can sleep," he says, pulling a sheet over us, but not before sliding over to me. He intertwines his legs in mine and wraps an arm around my waist, locking me into position.

"No one leaves tonight," he says and closes his eyes.

"No one leaves," I respond, and for the first time today, I feel like I can finally breathe.

I thought it was a dream, the pounding in my head, but the second I shift in bed I knew it isn't. Waves of nausea hit me as I slide off the bed and search the dark room for my clothes.

I can hear Sam shifting as I try to get my bearings. "No one leaves," he mumbles quietly, his voice full of sleep. I barely make out what he's saying against the constant thud in my head.

"Sam," I cry out, falling to my knees. Crashing down on the floor with the force of my entire weight, I crumble and begin to cry.

"Kate." I hear him kicking the sheets off of him, and I hold my head between my hands. I haven't had one this bad in a long time. "What's wrong?" he asks, his tone becoming anxious as he pulls me up off the floor.

Between gasping breaths, I'm able to tell him where to find the medicine I need. In a flurry of activity, I hear him run out of the room, a few seconds later the front door slamming behind him. What must've been less than a minute, but felt more like an hour, Sam is back. Even though I can tell he has the lights on, my headaches cause temporary vision loss. I can make out large objects, but not details. I can see Sam next to me and make out the bed just off to my left.

"What do I do?" he asks, sitting down next to me.

"The plastic case," I tell him, and he hands it to me. I'm so used to giving myself injections that, within seconds, I'm pressing the injectable syringe to my thigh and pushing the button to deliver the pain medicine I need to help me cope with these debilitating headaches.

With a snap, the needle hits my thighs and I begin counting to five hundred. It takes about five minutes for the medicine to begin offering relief. When I get to thirty, I ask Sam for water, and I hear him rush from the room and return with a glass.

By the time I get to one hundred and eighty, I've taken the anti-nausea medication that I pray will keep me from vomiting on Sam's floor. "Give me about five minutes," I tell him, and he sits down next to me. I can feel his worry as he pulls me closer to him, covering me with a bed sheet as he rests his back against the end of the bed. He does his best to tuck the sheet around me without trying to move me. My heart rate decreases as the pain begins to lessen, and my muscles are relaxing as well.

The pounding is still there, but it's beginning to minimize when I finally stop counting at three hundred and eighty-four in my head.

I try to push myself up, but Sam stops me. "Don't move," he says as he starts to stand. He slides his hands under me and carefully lifts me, the sheet falling off of me and to the floor below. He walks us cautiously around the end of the bed and lays me gently back in the spot I left about ten minutes ago.

"What just happened?" he asks, shutting off the bedroom light. The entire bed shifts when he crawls back in next to me. I allow myself to curl into him. His grasp is protective and strong. His heart beats wildly against my back, and his thighs curl just under my bottom.

"I get headaches," I begin, just above a whisper. It still hurts to talk, which is normal. I pause, trying to focus on breathing and the incessant pounding that is still wracking my head. "I need sleep," I mumble, the medicine clearly making me drowsy.

"Then sleep," he says, pressing a kiss to the back of my head. He holds me in a vise like grip, as if he's afraid I'll vanish into thin air. His arms are comforting and exactly what I need right now.

When I wake up, the sun is barely peeking through the drawn curtains in Sam's room. The bed is empty next to me as I rub my temples. My clothes are nowhere to be found so I wrap myself in the bed sheet that's still sitting on the floor from last night, or early this morning, whenever my headache came on.

I hear Sam's voice as I open his bedroom door and walk down the short hallway out to the living area and kitchen. Sam is standing at the large island in a pair of athletic shorts, his chest bare and his cell phone pressed to his ear. His eyes follow me as I approach him.

"Ten clubs that we know of," he says before he stops abruptly. "Can I call you back? I have to take care of something here."

I run my hand across the cold stone counter as I wait for him to end his call. His eyes never leave me, and they tell me he's concerned.

"Thanks." he says, tossing his phone on a stack of folders in front of him. "How're you feeling?" he asks, stepping up to me and reaching for my hands. He pulls me closer to him and I oblige.

"Better." I take a deep breath. "What time is it?" I glance outside at the bright sun.

"Ten-thirty."

I gasp. "Sam! Why didn't you wake me up? I have to work!" I pull out of his grasp.

He shakes his head and reaches out, stopping me as I move to leave. "Not today, Kate. I talked to Nick. He called someone." Sam's shoulders rise, and he steps in front of me blocking my escape.

"Adam?" I ask, frowning.

"Yes! Adam," he confirms. "Nick told him you were under the weather and taking the day off. Adam said 'thank fuck' because apparently you're a workaholic and never take time off." He raises his eyebrows and waits for my reaction.

I roll my eyes, still feeling a dull pain in the back of my head. "I'll just go in for a half-day," I tell Sam, trying to shrug out of his grasp.

"Nope. You have strict orders." He smirks.

"From who?" I narrow my eyes, anxious to see whose orders I'm following. I don't like being told what to do.

"From me." He runs his thumbs up and down my bare forearms, not letting me out of his hold.

"And who do you think you are?" I cock my head and purse my lips, trying not to smile.

He leans in, pressing a light kiss to my lips. "Who do you want me to be, Kate?" His warm breath causes a shiver to run up my spine.

I gasp loudly, pulling away from him. "What did you tell Nick? Oh my god, did you tell him I stayed with you?"

Looking amused, Sam responds, "Actually, he didn't ask any questions. I'm going to assume," he makes air quotes with his fingers, "that he thinks his little sister is old enough to make decisions about where and with whom she spends the night."

"He'll fire you," I snap at him.

But Sam is unfazed as he laughs at me. "He's not going to fire me."

"You don't know my brother." I shake my head. Nick has

never intervened in my past relationships, but I cannot believe he'd want me sleeping with his newest employee.

"Kate. Calm down. Nick is a smart man. I'm going to bet he was able to deduce the situation. His only concern was for you."

I let out a long sigh. "Fine. But don't get too comfortable here. He'll probably transfer you to New York by the end of the week."

Sam laughs again, pulling me into his arms, and presses a kiss to my temple.

"Well then, you better start packing," he whispers against my forehead.

TWELVE

"So talk to me about the headaches," I tell Kate as my thumb taps the steering wheel.

She sits in the passenger seat of my car, her body angled toward me with her head resting on the back of the seat. Two days ago, Kate scared the living shit out of me with her headache episode, and she's been reluctant to talk to me about it. I now have her trapped in my car for an almost thirty minute commute to her friend Adam's house for a barbecue, and I'm going to force some damn answers out of her.

"It's not a big deal, Sam." She sighs heavily. That's been her go-to answer every time I've asked her about it.

"Bullshit." I chance a glance at her. Her eyes are downcast, and she's pulled her bottom lip in between her teeth. I hate the vulnerability I see, but I need to know. "You scared me."

"I'm sorry," she says, reaching out and placing her hand on my arm.

"Just talk to me. I need to understand what you're dealing with, so I understand what *we're* dealing with." It's a bold statement, but I don't give a shit. If I can help her, I will.

She pulls her hand back and laces it through her other, placing them both in her lap, her sign of retreat. "I don't know what to tell you," she says softly. "They started about a year ago. At first I thought it was because I needed glasses, so I had my eyes checked and that wasn't it." She pauses. "But over the last six months, they've increased in severity, so my doctor wants me to have an MRI."

Merging onto the freeway, I look over to Kate again. Her fingers are twisted so tightly together they're turning red.

I grip the steering wheel harder as I think about what could be the cause of her headaches. "So we'll do the MRI. When is it scheduled for?"

"*We'll* do the MRI?" She smirks at me.

I find no humor in this conversation. What happened the other night was serious and scared the shit out of me. "Yes. *We'll* do the MRI. I want to be there for you, Kate. If you'll let me."

Her smirk becomes a serious smile as she tucks a strand of hair behind her ear. "I'd like that. A lot," she says, turning to look out the passenger window. Then her smile fades as I lose her to her thoughts, her own internal battle as to what's causing them.

"Everything's going to be fine," I tell her, laying my hand on her thigh. "You've probably got a pinched nerve in your neck or something like that." I try to shrug off the seriousness of the situation and lighten the mood, but I can see fear written across her face. "Hey." I reach for her chin and turn her head toward me. "I mean it. Everything is going to be just fine."

"Okay," she says with a short nod.

"So what do I need to know about Adam?" I change the topic.

Kate shifts in her seat and turns back to me. "He's my best friend," she deadpans. My stomach turns when she says that.

Best friend? "He's married to Melissa, she's the greatest." She smiles. "And they have the sweetest little baby boy, Mason."

My stomach suddenly calms as she tells me what a great family man Adam is and how much she likes Melissa. We pull up to the bungalow style house, and Kate oohs and awes over the neighborhood. Apparently, she loves these southern style homes and points out architectural features as they differ from house to house. Her eye for detail is like none other.

With a bottle of wine in one hand and Kate's hand in my other, we maneuver the walkway and up the three stairs to the front door. Just as we approach, the door springs open and there stands a woman holding a baby and swaying from hip to hip.

"Kate," she says with a large smile. "I'm so, so glad you came. We're outnumbered. Adam's old fraternity buddies are in the backyard wanting to relive their glory days...tonight... at my house!" She sounds exasperated, and her eyes bulge as she continues to sway. "I have a bad feeling a keg and hookers are going to show up in a couple of hours!" she says with a laugh.

"Boys!" Kate chides, laughing before she immediately reaches for the baby boy in Melissa's arms. She handles that baby with such ease, propping him up on her shoulder as Melissa reaches out for my hand.

"I'm Melissa," she says with a sincere smile.

"I'm sorry, I should've introduced you," Kate says, and she kisses the chubby cheek of the baby in her arms. "But I couldn't wait to get my hands on this little nugget!" Kate begins walking with a little bounce in her step, cooing at the little bundle in her arms, and I take Melissa's hand for a shake.

"Sam Cortez," I offer. "Since it appears we'll be chugging beer tonight, I'm going to assume that wine is a bit overstated?" I joke, handing her the bottle of merlot.

"Beer for those hooligans." She rolls her eyes, using her thumb to point toward what I assume is the backyard.

"But Kate and I will enjoy this!" She holds the bottle up and gives it a little shake. "Come on." She waves at me to follow her. "Guys are this way." We walk through the small living room and into a large kitchen. The entire house looks recently remodeled. Nothing fancy or over the top, but simple and clean.

Just off the back of the kitchen is an open sliding glass door leading out to a wooden deck. Four guys are standing around, drinking beers and laughing. Kate steps outside, still cuddling that baby in her arms and walks up to the group of men. A man I presume is Adam leans in and one-arm hugs her, pressing his lips to the baby's head.

I follow Kate and Adam peers at me over Kate's shoulder. "Going to introduce us?" he says, nudging Kate.

She rolls her eyes at him, and I can't help but grin. Adam is nothing that I had expected him to be. He's medium height and build, normal-looking in an 'I wouldn't notice him on the street' kind of way.

"Sam Cortez," I reach my hand out to him before Kate even has a chance to introduce us.

"Adam Anderson." He shakes my hand in return. Even a common name. Nothing strikes me as threatening about him, and I instantly put any of my hesitations about him being Kate's best friend to bed.

"Nice to meet you," I start. "I've heard a lot about you." I notice Kate's smile growing as Adam and I talk.

"Beer?" he offers, looking around for the cooler.

"Ah, yeah...please."

He walks to the edge of the deck and pulls a bottle of beer from the cooler, handing it to me when he returns. "I'm glad you could join us." He looks over to Kate, who's still swaying from hip to hip with the baby tucked safely in her arms. She looks beautiful holding a baby, so natural. "So Kate tells me you work with Nick." He looks to Kate and then back to me.

"Yep." I nod my head, taking a sip of cool beer. "Just transferred here from Phoenix."

"Why?" he asks and I go still.

Kate stops swaying, giving Adam a hardened look. She shakes her head a little bit, causing him to shrug, and I wonder what's been said about me prior to this conversation.

I shake off the uneasiness settling between us and tell him the truth. "Was just time for a change. I grew up in Phoenix, went to college in Phoenix, started my career in Phoenix...it was time to get out—time for a fresh start." I press the beer bottle to my lips and take a long pull as I watch Adam absorb what I've told him.

He looks at me skeptically and back to Kate as he continues. "Well, you chose the right place to move. It's amazing here!"

Kate visibly relaxes as Adam tells me all about the weather, the beach, and everything he likes to do outdoors. He actually sounds like a pretty cool guy, someone I could see myself hanging out with. Walking over, Kate stands next to me just as Melissa arrives with a glass of wine.

"Hold this, will you?" Melissa hands the glass to me and takes the now sleeping baby from Kate's arms. "You're a baby whisperer. He's been so fussy lately." She arranges the little guy in her arms before turning around to take the baby inside.

"I love that little boy," Kate tells me as she watches Melissa disappear with him.

"He's a cute kid," I remark.

"Thanks," Adam says, taking a drink of his own beer. "He looks like me."

Kate rolls her eyes and both Adam and I laugh. Kate pulls

the wine glass from my hand and walks away, leaving Adam and I alone as she introduces herself to the three men who Adam was speaking with a few minutes ago. I love how outgoing she is…even when I know she'd prefer not to be. She has this comforting air about her, and everyone who meets her instantly warms up to her.

"So you and Kate," Adam says candidly, rocking back and forth from heel to toe.

I glance at him out of the corner of my eye. "What about us?" I ask, sounding a bit defensive.

He takes a deep breath. "I mean…she's—"

"You don't have to worry about her, Adam." I try to say it without sounding like a dick. "I like her. I have no intentions of hurting her."

He instantly stops rocking and smiles at me. "It's not her I'm worried about," he says, letting out a small laugh. "She goes through men faster than she goes through shoes. Three, four a month. You should hear the stories…"

My stomach drops, and I'm sure the look on my face says exactly what I'm feeling.

"I'm just kidding, man!" He slaps me on the shoulder as he roars with laughter. "You should've seen your face."

I shake my head and finish the rest of my beer, handing him the empty bottle.

He tosses it into a plastic recycling container on the deck and continues. "But seriously, Sam. She's a great girl. A good friend." He clears his throat. "I just don't want to see her hurt," he says, sounding genuine.

"I don't either," I respond, my voice clipped. I don't know what he's alluding to, but I'm not going to hurt Kate. "And like I said, I have no intention of hurting her."

"Good," he says with a curt nod, ending our conversation. "Let's get you another beer."

The rest of the evening is spent laughing, relaxing by the large bonfire, and having a good time. Adam and Melissa's friends are great, and everyone has been very kind and welcoming to me and Kate, who's currently curled up next to me on a patio couch. Her head is resting on my shoulder, and her knees are tucked up underneath her as Adam tells us wild stories of his time at UCLA. Melissa and Kate giggle periodically as Melissa rolls her eyes at the exaggerated stories these guys are sharing.

Kate turns her head to look at me and presses a sweet kiss to the side of my mouth. I run my fingers through her hair and, for a brief moment, I realize that this is what peace feels like. It's calm and happiness. It's comfortable and understated. It's sitting on an outdoor couch with the woman you're falling for, under the stars, and not wanting to be anywhere else in the world or with anyone else. That feeling that everything you simply need is right here in this very moment of time—that's peace.

Kate pushes herself up and leans in. "Will you take me home now?" Her eyes are sleepy, yet there's an underlying hunger in them. A hunger I want to explore—but I'm worried about her health.

"I never thought you'd ask." I wink at her, and she smiles, folding the blanket she was using while we both say our goodbyes to Adam and his friends, as well as Melissa, for the most enjoyable evening. It was nice to sit and talk and laugh and eat, but it was more important for me to meet Adam, and I'm so grateful she has a good friend in him. I like him and have put all of my hesitations about him and Kate aside.

Adam and Melissa walk us out to the car. Adam shakes my hand firmly, thanking us for coming, and he offers Kate a brief hug. Melissa and Kate whisper and giggle, and when Melissa's eyes keep shifting to me, I know I am their topic of conversation.

"Wine makes you two so fucking obvious!" Adam says, hooking his arm in Melissa's as he tries to drag her away. "Stop ogling the man, Melissa," Adam says with a headshake. Melissa and Kate laugh.

"Wine is my best friend!" Kate hollers back at him as both ladies continue to laugh. Adam finally drags Melissa back into the house, and I open the car door for Kate. She slides into the front seat like she's always belonged there. She smiles at me through the windshield as I make my way around the car and into the driver's seat.

Before I can start the car, Kate leans over the center console to kiss me. Pressing her soft lips to mine, she slips her palm over my dick, causing it to harden. Fuck, she could breathe on me and turn me on.

"Kate," I mumble against her lips.

"Sam," she sighs between kisses as she crawls over the console and straddles me. She reaches down between the seat and the door, finding the switch, and suddenly the seat begins to move backward. The street is dark and thank god it's a quiet street with no traffic.

My hands instinctively slide up her dress, brushing the sides of her thighs before palming her ass.

"No panties!" I hiss as my fingers glide across her smooth ass. She giggles against my lips and grinds her hips against mine. "Kate!" I warn her, and she grinds harder. "We're taking it slow tonight," I tell her. I'm still worried about her headache episode from a couple of nights ago, and I don't have as many answers as I do questions as she's not willingly divulging information that I keep requesting.

"I hate slow," she breathes in my ear as she kisses my neck.

"Kate!" I growl at her again.

"Fine, if you insist," she pouts, sliding off my lap and back into her seat. I immediately hate the absence of her body on mine but I'm worried about her.

I readjust my seat and start the car. As we drive home, Kate settles comfortably into her seat, and I can't help but smile. "Can I ask you something?" I glance at her and she smiles.

"Always."

"Are we moving too fast? Because if we are—"

She cuts me off. "Is this because of the other night?" She sits up straighter and adjusts her dress to cover more of her legs.

"No. This has nothing to do with the other night. I just want to make sure you're comfortable with the pace we're handling this."

"*This*?" She raises her eyebrows.

"Yes, *this*," I respond.

"What is *this*?" she asks, turning her body and full attention toward me.

I take a deep breath. "What do you want it to be?" I turn my attention back and forth between the road and Kate.

She shrugs slightly. "What do *you* want it to be?" She's avoiding my question.

"Right now, I want it to be what it is." I can see she's disappointed in my answer, but I continue anyway. "What we have is perfect." I turn and smile at her. "We may have started out a little unconventional, a little faster than I normally would, but, Kate, when you have the connection that you and I have, sometimes you have to throw out the rules and just roll with what's happening."

I see her swallow hard before the corners of her lips turn up into a full smile. "I love that answer," she says. "So let's roll with it, okay?"

I nod and smile. "Let's roll with it."

THIRTEEN

Kate

"I knew this was going to happen!" Nick barks at me through the other end of the phone. I pinch my eyes closed and hold my breath as he scoffs at me. "So what happens when this one doesn't work out, Kate!" he bites. "Because I shouldn't have to choose between my sister and my best goddamn employee."

I roll my eyes at my brother, not that he can see it through the other end of the phone. "No one's making you choose anything, Jesus, Nick. You're being a bit dramatic."

"Dramatic?" he huffs.

"I see you what, maybe once a month, Nick? And that's when I make the effort to go to you. I love you and Nic and the boys. I make the effort, Nick. I'm not saying this to upset you, but I want you to support me and what I want for once. So if this doesn't take off with me and Sam, there's no one to choose. Sam works for you, and he will continue to, and I'm your sister, and I always will be. If you're that pissed at me, choose Sam. You can toss a gift card at me for Christmas, sing Happy Birthday to me in October, and have me over for the kids' birthdays in the summer and your requirements as a dutiful brother are done." I've worn a path in the hardwood flooring as I circle the kitchen island in frustration.

"Screw you, Kate."

"No, Nick. Screw. You. You don't get to tell me who I can or cannot date." Nick has never cared who I've dated, slept with, or been in a relationship with ever. He's always been protective, but I know his anger is directed at me because it's Sam. If it were anyone else, this wouldn't even be a conversation between us.

Angrily he responds. "You're right. I can't. I just didn't think you'd jump in the sack with Sam a week after you met him."

"You're an asshole, you know that?" I'm so angry I'm literally shaking. My hands tremble, and my knees nearly knock together as I seethe. I called Nick to give him the courtesy of knowing what was happening between me and Sam. I didn't want him to find out unexpectedly or take out any of his concerns on Sam. I explained it was simple...casual...nothing serious...*yet*.

Of course, Nick being overprotective and overbearing Nick, he flipped his shit the second I breathed the name, "Sam."

I hear Nick let out a long sigh as I bite my tongue from saying anything more to my brother. I place a hand on the granite countertop to steady myself and stop my hand from shaking as I try to calm myself down before I say anything I will regret.

"I'm sorry," he finally says apologetically. "You're a grown woman and I shouldn't have said anything to—"

"Apology accepted," I cut him off before he has the chance to twist his apology into another scathing response. "Nick, I promise this won't get in the way of Sam's job. And I promise that if it doesn't work out with us, I would never expect you to make a decision between us."

His voice hitches with irritation. "It just muddies the lines—"

"Nick, I got it. We're all adults. We're going to manage this just fine," I answer him curtly.

He mumbles something under his breath, and then continues, "I'm just glad his ass is going to be occupied for the foreseeable future with this case." He continues talking, but I zone out. While it's not really the 'blessing' I was looking for, I'm relieved that my relationship with Sam is no longer something I need to hide from Nick.

Suddenly, his tone changes. "Hey, Kate, I gotta run. Let's catch up later, okay?"

"Sounds good, and Nick?"

"Yeah, sis?"

"Thank you."

Nick is quiet for a moment before clearing his throat. "I just want you to be happy."

I can hear the resolve in Nick's voice, and I can't fight the smile spreading across my face. "I am. I really am."

For the past week, Sam has been buried in work. I haven't seen him in five days. He sent me a brief text and said that Nick had him traveling for work and that he misses me and has been thinking of me. Every night I go home and wonder if this is the night he'll be coming home. I've learned over the years, from Nick and his work with the ATF, that you can't ask questions. That when they're working a case, their minds are useless for anything else—and that any distractions are dangerous. As hard as it is, their safety is of the utmost importance and I respect and appreciate that.

However, selfishly I'm annoyed because I want Sam with me. Yet the professional in me understands his job commitment and I admire Sam's devotion to his career. It's one of the things that attracted me to him, along with basically every single inch of his body.

I pound away at my keyboard, striking text in these contracts that I won't sign until they're perfect. I'm a perfectionist when it comes to my job, and I'm thankful I have something to spend my time working on so that I stop worrying and wondering about Sam.

Adam has been gone this week as well, so not only am I lonely at home, I've been lonely at work as well. Today was his first day back and he's either been extremely busy, or he's been avoiding me—as my instant messages and emails to him went unanswered. There's a soft knock on my office door before it slowly opens. To my surprise, it's Adam.

"There you are," I say, standing up to give him a quick hug. I feel him tense slightly and pull away. "What's wrong?" I take a seat back in my chair searching his face for answers. Adam takes the chair just across my desk and props his foot up on his opposite knee. "Tell me there is not more work coming," I pat the stack of contracts piling up on my desk. "We just can't handle it."

He shakes his head and swallows hard. "Just how serious are you and Sam?" he asks. Wow, no beating around the bush.

"Define serious," I say with a cautious smile, not even sure how to answer this question. My heart rate begins to pick up as he shifts in his seat, his posture taught.

"Dammit, Kate. This isn't a joke," he snaps at me, raking his hand over his face.

I wince as he snaps at me. "Jeez, I don't know. Why're you getting so defensive?" I push myself back from the desk a little bit, putting greater distance between us. Adam's eyebrows are furrowed, and he balls his hand into a tight fist. "What's going on, Adam?" I ask, my heart rate beginning to pick up once I really see how upset he is.

"I don't know," he says, rubbing his forehead and blowing a puff of air from his mouth. "I got some information on your boyfriend, and I don't know whether it's a big deal or not, but I'm fucking pissed off." He stops for a second and looks across the desk at me. "I fucking told him I didn't want to see you get hurt."

"Tell me." I sit up taller and straighten my shoulders, bracing myself for whatever bomb he's about to drop.

"When's the last time you *saw* him?" Adam asks sternly. And by *saw* him, I know he means 'slept with him'.

I wring my fingers together tightly. "Last week. Why? What the fuck is going on, Adam? You're scaring me." My voice hitches, and I can feel my emotions bubbling just under the surface.

Adam sighs and looks directly at me. "You know Marc, my college roommate, the guy that was at my house for the barbecue?" I nod my head quickly, feeling my throat go dry as he continues. From the look on Adam's face and the tone of his voice, I know what he's about to tell me can't be positive. "He happened to see Sam..." he pauses and takes a short breath, "with another woman."

My stomach drops. "What do you mean saw him with another woman? Marc lives in San Diego." My palms are beginning to sweat.

"They were going into an apartment, Kate. Late in the evening. Marc was pretty damn convinced she was a hooker."

"A hooker?" I blurt out and almost laugh. Shaking my head,

I respond snarkily, "I can tell you Sam has no need for a prostitute, Adam. He must be there for work."

Adam shakes his head. "Kate." His voice is hard, and his eyes tell me he's concerned.

"What?"

Adam rubs his face and leans in, pressing his elbows to my desk. "Marc said Sam stayed with her all night. He saw him leave in the morning. He stayed in another woman's apartment all night."

My stomach sinks, and my heart races. I swallow down the bile I feel rising in the back of my throat. "He just..." My voice breaks, and I bite my bottom lip to stop it from quivering.

"I don't know what he's told you, Kate...but staying at another woman's apartment hardly passes for work. And I don't know what ATF agents do, but I can't assume that he'd stay in an apartment with a barely dressed woman." Tears sting my eyes, and my lips quiver uncontrollably. Adam's face falls and his eyes are sympathetic when he sees me becoming visibly upset. "I didn't want to tell you, Kate, because you're my best friend and I didn't want to see you hurting...but goddammit, I *had* to tell you *because* you're my best friend, and I can't let you date some fucking piece of shit that's going to go behind your back—and with someone who is possibly a prostitute. Who the fuck does that?" He leans forward, resting his elbows on his knees.

Silence passes between us for a long moment while I wipe my wet cheeks with the back of my hand. "There has to be a reason," I say, almost defending him. "This doesn't make sense." My mind races, trying to recall all of our conversations, searching for any clue as to what he's up to. Unless I don't really know who Sam Cortez is. Unless he's playing me.

I reach for my phone and immediately text Nick: *Where's*

Sam? I wait for a reply, but nothing comes in. My heart races as more doubts fill my mind, and I now wonder if Sam really is working.

I text Sam next: *Where are you?* Again, no reply.

"If I see him, I'm going to kill him," Adam says, his voice laced with anger. "Something didn't sit right with me the other night when I met him...and I couldn't place my finger on it, Kate—"

With a shaky voice I try to calm the situation until I get answers. "Don't judge him—yet. Let me find out what's going on." My heart is racing, and my mind is all over the place as I try to reference what Nick has told me with what Sam has told me, and it's all just too much. Emotions take over again, and I lay my head down on my desk and cry.

Adam stays with me while I cry and question everything, including myself. I thought I was a better judge of character, but I guess the saying is true—you never really know who someone is.

FOURTEEN

I haven't seen Kate in seven days, and I'm dying to get back to her...see her, sink into her. I've been fighting off thoughts of her soft body under mine for days. Thinking of being inside her has me practically hard, and I've had to focus on work. I've been holed up in this shitty apartment while we do surveillance on the strip club across the street.

"Cortez," Agent Beck hollers from the living room where our command center is all set up. "You know that bug that Ramos got in the office over at the club?"

I nod and walk over to the table where Agent Beck is listening to audio from the recording device Agent Ramos was able to get into the business office of the strip club we're surveilling. "It picked up a conversation and we got it all on tape." He smiles victoriously, keeping a headphone pressed to his ear.

"What does it say?" I lean in and press both of my hands to the top of the wood table where he's frantically scribbling notes in a spiral notebook. I work old school. I jot my notes on paper before transferring my final work into the computer that holds all the case information and can be accessed by the agency in any location.

"Navarro is transporting the guns into the U.S. via Nogales. They're coming in from Colombia via Russia. Three shipments in the next thirty days. Destination in Mexico is unknown. I couldn't pick that up from the audio. The drugs are coming up to us through TJ." He taps his pen on the notepad and looks up at me, a pleased look on his face.

We're all excited and the mood in the room has shifted with this news. "You got ID on the narcotics?"

"Coke."

"Any idea where they're headed?" If I know Navarro and his distribution network like I think I do, my bet is they'll land in San Diego, Vegas, Denver, Omaha, and Minneapolis. His distribution channel is big on the West coast and Midwest.

"Midwest, most likely." He shrugs.

"Yes! I knew it." I smack Agent Beck on the back. "Ramos is at the club tonight. We'll see if she was able to get any other intel when she gets back here." I glance at the watch on my wrist and see that it's almost midnight. Agent Ramos won't be back until almost three in the morning, so I've got three hours to get notes put together with the intel that we've already collected.

Leslie Ramos is one of Los Angeles's newest ATF agents. She volunteered to go undercover in one of Navarro's U.S. based strip clubs to see if we could get any intelligence into the moving of the firearms and drugs we're seeing go across the U.S./ Mexican border. He's been using the strip clubs as a cover to move the guns and drugs. I'm over the fucking moon that we're finally getting our first taste of what's going on behind those club doors.

"Who's with Ramos?" I ask, wondering who the two agents are that are assigned to her tonight. We have plainclothes agents inside, watching Ramos to ensure her safety, as well as bringing back any valuable intel that they see or hear that Ramos may or may not be privy to. They pose as regular customers, yet are invaluable to Ramos and us.

"Landers and Hart."

I nod again with confirmation that two of our best are inside with Ramos.

Being undercover is a tricky game. We have to dot our I's and cross our T's to ensure no one fucks up. If Landers and Hart leave too quickly after Ramos, it looks suspicious. Professional criminals know behaviors to look for, therefore we always need to be one step ahead.

As I wait for Ramos, Hart, and Landers to return and brief us, I pull out my phone and send Kate another text. She hasn't responded to the last two I've sent. She texted me two days ago, asking where I was, and I couldn't tell her. Once this case is over, I can share some details with her, but while we're actively working it, I cannot say anything about what I'm working on or where I'm at. This is for her safety and for mine, as well as a strict agency policy.

I sense her pulling back, and I can understand why. Being with someone who, for days and sometimes weeks at a time, is completely removed from reality while we work on these cases, can't be easy. However, since Nick has been doing this, I was under the assumption she understood what came with me being a special agent for the ATF.

I busy myself with case notes and review my file over and over, looking for anything that could provide more details on the guns moving through our border and into Mexico. AK-47s and various other assault rifles are a hot commodity south of the border.

Just as I close the file, the apartment door opens and in

walks Agent Ramos in a pair of too-short cut-off jean shorts and a tank top. She grabs an oversized sweatshirt off the chair and pulls it over her head to cover herself up as she sits down at the table where we've all gathered.

"I got the bug in place." She grins and grabs a tissue from the Kleenex box on the table to wipe some of the excess makeup from her face.

"We heard," Agent Beck says excitedly. "We've already got confirmed intel on shipments moving to and from the border." Agent Ramos's eyes widen, and she looks at me.

"Great job, Ramos. I don't know how you got in there so quickly, but great work. Really." I roll my fingers across the table just as the apartment door opens again and in walks Hart and Landers.

If I didn't know these two men, I'd never in a million years guess they were federal agents. Landers looks like he's a twenty-one-year-old fraternity boy with tanned skin and bleach blond hair. Your typical Southern California pretty boy. And Hart, he looks like a kid who's been stuck in a skate park for the last ten years with shaggy hair and grungy clothes.

It's all part of the role. These agents are the best. They're able to transform into anything we need. Drug dealer? Easy. Surfer? Piece of cake. Stripper? Not a problem. I look at Leslie Ramos, who is clearly happy to be back and covered up. I've been put in situations that have made me very uncomfortable over the years, but never once have I had to put myself out there like she has on this case.

It's one thing to pose as something, it's another to actually take your clothes off and perform like it's your job. I couldn't be more proud of her—and protective at the same time. Landers and Hart are the epitome of professional, and I couldn't be happier that those two are in the club with her tonight.

We have a great group of men and women in the Los Angeles office, and I know I've made the right decision to transfer here.

Agent Beck briefs the team on the details they've been able to pull off the audio. Agents Hart, Landers, and Ramos listen intently as the group discusses strategies to see how we can get more information to help us build a tighter case. The strip club is just a front for the business. The money travels in and out of the club, but the guns and drugs don't. However, the manager of the strip club, Tease, is one of Navarro's right hand men here in the states and is an invaluable resource to us—if we can get more information. He knows how and when the guns and drugs move, as we've heard from the audio we've captured coming from his office.

"What do you need me to do?" Ramos asks, pulling her knees up to her chest in a protective manner. I want to tell her she's done more than enough, but the truth is we need her.

Agent Hart clears his throat and looks at Ramos before turning to me. "Navarro has her in the front. Landers and I identified Dominguez, Castro, and Cano coming in and going to the private room in the back." Hart looks at Ramos again, whose eyes are downcast and focused on her hands wrapped tightly around her knees.

"No." I shake my head. "I won't send her in there all alone." The back room is a private dance area where the dancers are totally nude. In most clubs, anyone can go to the private room, provided there's space. In Navarro's club, it's invite only. They're also breaking the law by allowing alcohol in the private room. California law does not allow alcohol in the fully nude clubs or fully nude areas in strip clubs.

Ramos has been working the topless area, which has been uncomfortable enough for all of us. I can't for the sake of her safety send her to the back without our guys within arm's reach should something happen.

"It might be our only—"

"No!" I snap at Agent Hart, startling everyone at the table. Silence falls across the room as I strategize our next steps.

"I'll do it." Leslie's voice is meek. "It's the only way to find out what's happening back there," she says, dropping her legs to the floor and sitting up straight. "I'll ask Navarro if I can try it— just for one night. See if I can get a bug in there." She looks around the table as all of us men sit quietly, letting her speak. "Am I nervous? Yes. Do I want to bring these assholes down? Hell, yes." That elicits a smirk from Agent Hart and a smile from Agent Landers. Those three have been relentless in their pursuit of the Navarro cartel.

I nod as a plan formulates in my head. "Landers and Hart. You're out for tonight. Go home. Rest. And we'll see you tomorrow. I'll go in and I'll bring Marcus, Jackson, and McMillian. We're going under the ruse of a happy hour. I want everyone dressed like they've come from an office. We'll be in the front room." I look at Ramos, who nods.

I can't send Hart and Landers back in for a second day without it looking suspicious. Security there is top notch, and they know who comes and goes, who's new and what doesn't sit right. A group of four coworkers doesn't look as suspicious as two guys back for a second night.

With a plan in motion, I send the team back to their hotels to catch some sleep. Ramos stays behind as I gather a few of my belongings and toss them into my bag.

"You sure you're okay with this?" I ask as she tugs at the hem of her oversized sweatshirt. It's so big it covers up her short jean shorts. Her feet are stuffed into a pair of Converse sneakers, and her long hair is piled on top of her head. She looks so young, so vulnerable, and guilt floods me as I think of putting her in a position of danger.

She's a young agent. A good agent, but she doesn't have the years of experience under her belt for a case like this. "Yeah," she says with a small smile.

"You won't be wired," I remind her. Not many places to hide equipment when your attire is your birthday suit. "I might be able to find some earrings."

"It's fine," she insists. "Just tell me where you want me to place the bug." She's drawn us an entire map of the club, from the all-nude communal room to the smaller private rooms in the back. She's drawn every table, chair, window, rest room, etc. We've got devices the size of a dime placed in various rooms throughout the club, and we need to get to just a few more places. However, ensuring her safety is more important.

"Les," I call her and she looks up at me. "If you're uncomfortable at any time, I need you to tell me. Promise."

She smiles at me stoically. "Promise." She knows the dangers of this job, and I trust her professional judgment.

"Good. Let's go. I'll walk you out." I pull my phone from my pocket to check the time. Four twenty-seven in the morning… and still no response from Kate.

FIFTEEN

Kate

Waking up with a headache is not how I wanted to start my day. I know that the added stress I'm putting on myself in regards to Sam is not helping me. I stumble through my morning routine, barely keeping it together. I feel terrible, but I know I need to get to work and push through it.

By the time I get myself halfway put together and into the car, my headache seems to be letting up slightly. I manage through traffic with my coffee and make it to my office to find Adam waiting for me... with that same look plastered to his face that I saw the other day. The look telling me he's pissed and concerned but mostly worried.

"You don't look good," he says as I step into my office and drop my purse on my desk.

"Well, good morning to you, too," I mutter.

"Sorry." He cringes and sits down in the chair. I take my time getting situated and powering up my laptop while he shifts uncomfortably.

"I take it this visit isn't just to see how I'm doing," I guess, my voice monotone.

"Yes, it is," he says defensively.

I sigh. "Adam, do you think I don't know any better? You check on me by instant message every morning. You never stop in my office before noon because you're a grumpy morning person."

He lets out a deep sigh and nods, pulling his cell phone from his front pocket. He stares at the screen for a few moments before setting the sleek phone on my desk and sliding it across the wood where it stops in front of me.

The look on his face is sad, almost regretful when he points out the time the latest text message came in. "This morning. Four-thirty."

There, in a text message from Marc, is a picture of Sam and a young woman. A pretty woman. He's wearing a button up dress shirt with no tie. The sleeves have been rolled up. She's wearing a huge Michigan State sweatshirt that basically covers anything else she may have on. Her tan legs peek out from underneath the sweatshirt. She's looking up at Sam and smiling, and he's looking down on her. She's very petite next to his large frame.

There's nothing incriminating in this photo, other than that he's with a woman at four-thirty in the morning. He sent me a text message early this morning, a little past midnight, but I haven't responded to the last three he's sent. They've been short, vague, and not something I want to deal with right now. I want to talk to Sam, not accuse him of something.

"Say something," Adam urges me.

"What do you want me to say?" I slide the phone back to him, and he rakes his hands over his face. "Adam, I owe it to myself to speak to him about this. I don't want to make assumptions or get into something with him over the phone."

He stares at me in disbelief. From his perspective, this is

black and white. Sam's lying to me and I should let him go via a text message and move on.

"Look," I start. "Let me think about this a little bit. I have a terrible headache, and I just need to get these contracts done today." I point to the growing stack on my desk. "Let's grab lunch and just catch up. Talk about anything other than Sam." I offer my friend a sincere smile, and he begrudgingly returns it.

"Fine. I'll come and get you at twelve-thirty. But we're going to that deli that has that amazing matzo ball soup."

I can't help but let out a little laugh. "Deal."

As Adam stands up and walks across the office to let himself out, he stops just outside the door. He turns to look at me and smiles. "You deserve better, Kate," he says softly before he turns and disappears down the hall.

My stomach drops as the picture of Sam smiling down at the young brunette burns itself into my memory. I rub my temples, praying the medicine I've taken grabs a better hold because I feel like I'm losing my battle today.

By the time Adam makes his way to my office for lunch, I'm literally incapacitated. For the last two hours, I've tried to fight against the increasing pain taking over my head and now my entire body. My vision started blurring until I finally couldn't see anything in front of me, rendering me useless. I rest my pounding head on my hands. Even the slightest of sounds feels like someone is stabbing me in the head with a dull knife. If this is what death feels like, I hope I go quickly. I can't make out light or dark, and the intense pressure behind my eyes is overwhelming. It's taking everything in me to breathe through the nausea and focus on not fainting.

I can sense someone next to me, and I can feel Adam's hand on the back of my neck, gently squeezing. I hear his gentle voice speaking into my ear, but I have no idea what he's saying. Just knowing he's here brings me the slightest bit of comfort. Then, suddenly, the pain increases until I finally hear a pop inside my head and everything goes black.

SIXTEEN

"The list of charges I have documented fills damn near two pages!" I tell Nick over the phone. I tap the end of my pen excitedly on the legal pad in front of me. "It's unreal what these guys are moving."

He's quiet and doesn't respond. This is very unlike the Nick I've gotten to know so well.

I try to uncover what's behind his somber mood. "Soooo, ah—"

"Kate told me about you two," he interrupts me, suddenly going silent.

Shit. I wasn't expecting him to throw *that* at me. "I wanted to talk to you about that," I begin, raking my hand over my face. "But you sent me to San Diego and it wasn't a conversation I wanted to have on the phone. I feel like this warranted a face-to-face."

"You're damn right it did, which is why I'm so fucking pissed—"

I sigh, "Look, Nick—"

He cuts me off again. "I'm not happy about this, Cortez. I

don't like it. That's my sister. She's family. Don't fucking hurt her, Sam. She deserves the world, and if you're going to just fuck her over—"

Now it's my turn to interrupt him. We both can't seem to get a word in edgewise. "That won't happen. I like her. I more than like her, Nick. I care about her…and don't make me choose, or you're going to lose the best agent you've ever hired…because I'll choose Kate over this job any damn day of the week." My heart is pounding wildly, and I close my eyes, waiting for Nick's response. I can already envision him writing up my termination papers.

He exhales loudly. "I hope you'd choose her."

"In a heartbeat," I respond without a second thought. And suddenly, everything falls into place for me. She's my future. She's my motivation to move forward and leave the past behind me. She is what I've been missing. In my gut I knew this, but given the thought of choosing my job or her—it'd always be her.

"I'm glad we had this little talk," he says with an edge of sarcasm before turning back to business. "I've briefed everyone here in L.A. as to the progress on the case. No one can believe that you and Ramos have been able to gather the intelligence that you have in such a short period of time. Navarro is usually tight, Sam. He's getting sloppy. This worries me."

I nod in agreement and take a deep breath. "Me, too. Everything I've researched about him tells me he doesn't fuck up. We've been able to get bugs in three different areas of the club. That is almost unheard of. I want Ramos out of there, though. If shit is as messy as I think it might be, I don't want her in the crossfire."

"Agreed. The bugs are in place. Have her resign from the club; tell them she has family issues or something that's realistic. Have Hart and Landers make a trip back tomorrow to see if they notice anything off. Hart said he saw Castro in there. What the fuck is Castro doing in a club meeting with Navarro?"

"Good question. They met in the private room in the back. We didn't have a bug in there yet. If he comes back, and they meet in there again, we're ready to grab what we can."

"Good," he barks. "I'd like to see both of those fuckers go down. However, Navarro is our focus. He's got the guns. Let the DEA handle that fucking bastard, Castro."

"Castro and Navarro together make me nervous, though, Nick."

"Yeah, me, too. But you did exactly what I wanted you to do. The rest will fall into place. Get Ramos out of there, hang around for a couple more days and see what you can pick up. Sounds like the list of charges is enough, so if we don't get anything else, we'll move in and pick him up." I hear his cell phone ringing so he quickly lets me go.

I look at the notebook in front of me and smile at the list of charges we can bring against Navarro. A rush of adrenaline passes through me like it used to when I was working cases back in Phoenix. I was afraid that after the shooting I would never feel the rush again that I got when I was close to nailing a case. I'm glad to know I was wrong.

My cell phone rings again, and Nick's number flashes across my screen. "That was quick," I answer with a laugh.

His voice is direct and filled with a sense of urgency. "Sam. It's Kate. She's in an ambulance on her way to Cedars Sinai." The phone goes dead just as the news punches me in the fucking gut.

The California traffic never bothered me much until today. Until what is supposed to be a two-hour drive turns into nearly four. I've left voice messages for both Nick and Adam in hopes that someone will call me and update me on what the hell is happening. By the time I make it to Cedars Sinai, my patience is worn thin. When I finally see Adam in a waiting area outside the neurology department, I nearly breathe a sigh of relief.

"What happened?" I ask, rushing to his side.

His eyes narrow and he looks me over with an untrusting look. "She's in surgery," he says, turning his attention back to his phone.

"I've been trying to get a hold of you and Nick—"

He cuts me off, his voice angry. "Yeah, well, Nick's phone died, and I have no desire to talk to you."

"What the fuck is your problem, Adam?" I emphasize his name. "Because whether you like it or not, Kate is my girlfriend—"

"Is she?" he snaps, his face twisted in anger.

"Yes. She is." I'm certain and sure in my delivery. Fuck Adam and his questioning. Kate is mine.

"Was she your girlfriend when I received this picture of you leaving an apartment in San Diego with a woman who looks like a prostitute?" He shoves his cell phone in my face. It's a picture of me and Ramos leaving the apartment the department has us working out of.

I sigh loudly and rub my eyes. "I can't talk about that picture, Adam, but Kate, she *is* my girlfriend. No question about it. So I need you to stop rushing to conclusions about what you *think* you saw, and trust me."

"*Think* I saw?" The asshole barks and lets out a sarcastic laugh. "It's pretty fucking obvious what I saw. Stay the fuck away from Kate, or else—"

"Or else what?" I get in his face. "What are you going to do, Adam?"

He swallows hard and diverts his eyes to the nurse walking directly at us.

"You two need to keep it down," she says, eyeing both of us. "This is a hospital, not some backwoods bar."

I step away from Adam and apologize.

"I assume you're both here for Ms. Stevens," she says.

"Yes," we both say in unison, just as Nick comes jogging back down the corridor.

"You here for Ms. Stevens, too?" she asks Nick, who eagerly nods his head.

"Yes, I'm her brother."

"And who are these two?" She points her finger between Adam and I.

"Friend and..." Nick looks at me.

"Boyfriend," I answer, emphasizing the word for Adam.

"Well, I can only talk to family. Can you join me over in this private room?" She gestures to a door just down the hall. "I suggest you two take a breather and stay away from each other." She cocks an eyebrow and looks between us both. I'm not fucking going anywhere until Nick returns with some answers.

I pace the floor just outside the room the nurse and Nick are in. When the door opens, the nurse looks me up and down and shakes her head slightly before disappearing back down the hall.

I find Nick sitting in a chair, rubbing his temples. My stomach lurches, and I feel sick.

"Nick," I say, getting his attention. He waves me in and Adam is hot on my tail. Now is not the time for me to tell him to piss off because Kate means more to me than this piece of shit spewing bullshit he knows nothing about. "What's happening?"

Nick takes a deep breath and begins rattling off all kinds of things I don't understand. Brain tumor. Headaches. And on and on. It's when he pauses and tells us that the doctor is almost certain it's benign that all the anxiety I've been carrying around releases. I feel myself becoming overwhelmed with emotion and immediately step out of the room.

I don't cry. I never have. I've learned to bury my emotions deep inside and remain calm, cool, and collected at all times. Under pressure. When I'm sad. It's how I learned to cope during my childhood. It's what makes me a fucking great federal agent.

I walk down the hall, barely able to see through my blurred vision. Kate has to be okay. She *has* to. I don't dream, and I don't envision my future. I never have. I've always been a 'life is today' kind of guy. But now, when I let the faintest visions of my future seep in, Kate is there.

Nick finds me staring out a window at nothing at all. Lost within myself. "Sam," he says quietly, getting my attention. I turn to him, and he hands me a cup of coffee. "Looks like you could use this." I've been up for over thirty hours between the case and getting back to Los Angeles.

"Thanks, man." I take a sip of the simmering hot coffee. It burns the back of my throat, but I don't care.

"You okay?"

"I think so. I'm worried," I tell him honestly. "So goddamn worried."

"Me, too," he admits, his face weary and worn. He looks like he's been hit by a train.

"I just got her, I can't lose her."

Nick stands there watching me as I try to push down the emotions that have risen to the surface yet again.

"I love her," I finally admit, my voice breaking.

"I can see that," he says. We stand shoulder to shoulder,

staring out the hospital window in silence. "I'm sorry about giving you shit," he says quietly. "She's all the family I have left, and I'm a little overprotective of her."

"Rightfully so," I tell him. I can't fault him for being a good brother.

Nick turns and slaps me on the shoulder, a friendly gesture. "I'm going to head out. They said no visitors tonight, but tomorrow she can see us. I guess the procedure was non-invasive and she should be feeling okay. They only had to remove a small portion of her hair as well." he says that as a positive, and fuck I wasn't even thinking of her hair. Her gorgeous hair.

It doesn't matter. If she's okay, that's all I care about.

"Go get some rest," he says, "and let's meet back here in the morning."

I nod and take another sip of coffee as Nick turns to walk away.

"Hey, Sam?" he calls out to me. I turn to face him. "Just take good care of her." He nods and walks away.

"I will," I respond, even though he can't hear me.

SEVENTEEN

Kate

"I don't know who those two men are out there, but they've been at each other's throats since you've been in surgery," the nurse says to me as she checks the incision on my head. I can hear muffled voices and, at times, the raised voices, but I'm unable to make out whom the voices belong to.

"Who is it?" I ask her, realizing the hoarseness of my voice.

"Not your brother. I spoke with him yesterday. There is a really handsome one, tan skin, light brown hair…reminds me of William Levy. His smile is to die for."

"Sam," I whisper, closing my eyes.

"And the other one," she says, clicking her tongue. "He's a real piece of work. He's been instigating and prodding the other one all night long."

"They've been here all night?" I ask, shocked to hear this.

"Mmmhmm," she says. "That William Levy lookalike sat on the floor, propped against your door all night. Claims he's going to be the first one to see you this morning."

My heart leaps when the nurse tells me this. "He's a feisty one." She smirks.

"He is."

"And a damn good-looking one." She chuckles.

"I couldn't agree with you more." I try to clear my throat and push down some of the raspy sound that comes when I speak.

She changes out the saline on my IV bag, listens to my lungs, takes my blood pressure, and makes some notes on her laptop.

"For someone who had brain surgery yesterday, you're doing exceptionally well. I would ask that you keep your visit short and rest. You're going to be here for a few days to make sure there's no dangerous swelling or any other side effects. Sometimes it takes days for things to show up."

As she's wrapping things up, we can hear Sam and Adam bickering just outside the door. "I deserve hazard pay for dealing with those two," she says and winks at me. "Which one do you want me to send in first? The dreamboat?"

I try to laugh at her remark about Sam, but I'm still pretty groggy from the surgery. "Yes, please," I answer her.

"If you need anything, push the button on the side of the bed. I'm just down the hall."

"Thank you," I tell her.

She opens the door and Sam comes barreling through at the same time, darn near knocking her over.

"Kate," he says my name but not before the nurse puts her hand up and stops him dead in his track.

"Listen here, dreamboat," she says, and I almost choke on my laugh. Sam looks at me and back to the nurse bewildered. "She had brain surgery yesterday. She's recovering. And while it doesn't look bad on the outside, her incision is small, she had *brain surgery*." She emphasizes those last two words. "Keep it calm in here, and whatever drama you have going on out there," she points outside the door, "keep it there. Comprende?"

His lips turn up at the corners. "Understood."

She pats his chest and moves around him, shutting the door as she leaves. Sam stands with his dress shirt untucked and wrinkled. His hair is mussed, and he has dark circles under his eyes. The poor man looks like hell.

He wastes no time moving to me, pulling my hand gently into his, but with the conviction of a man who is determined. "Jesus, Kate." His voice breaks. "I was so worried..." He pauses, looking me over. He reaches an outstretched hand to touch me but retreats quickly.

"I'm okay," I tell him. "I'm going to be okay."

He swallows hard. "I wasn't ready to lose you...I never want to lose you, Kate." My heart beats frantically at his admission. He squeezes my hand, and his thumb rubs nervous circles on top of it. "I love you, Kate. I know it probably seems quick, but I do, I love you. Knowing you were in here and I couldn't do anything to help you—I couldn't hold you—it killed me, Kate."

Tears sting the backs of my eyes, and I take a deep breath.

"And before you say anything," he continues, "Adam showed me the photos...all the photos." He rolls his eyes. "Let me just say this...you know that in my line of work, during an active case, I cannot talk about any of it." He holds his gaze on mine. "When this case is closed, I'll be able to tell you everything. Just know, I'd never in a million years do *anything* to compromise our relationship."

I try to nod, but the pressure hurts. "I know," I answer him and wince. "I let my insecurities get the better of me, and I shouldn't have."

He sighs as I watch his mind piece it all together. "Is that why you weren't answering my texts?"

"Yeah," I admit, feeling foolish.

"Kate, we need to trust each other. I trust you implicitly." His eyes are sincere, and I realize I do trust him.

"And I promise to trust you."

"Good." He leans in and presses a long, gentle kiss to my forehead. "Now Adam is outside ready to kill me, and I haven't slept in forty-eight hours, so I'm going to go home and shower and come back. Visiting hours don't technically start for another," he looks at his watch, "thirty minutes, and Nick will be back. He's been beside himself."

"I'm sorry to scare all of you," I tell him. But, thankfully, we now know what was causing the headaches and we've got it taken care of.

"We all love you, Kate."

"I know." Tears well in my eyes as I'm so thankful for all the people that love and support me endlessly.

"I'll let Adam in. Talk some damn sense into that friend of yours…because I'll kick his ass into next year if he tries to come between us, Kate."

I muster up a small laugh. "I will. He just worries about me."

He raises his eyebrows. "Not his job. That's my job. And I swear on everything holy, I will not fail you." He sets my hand on the edge of the bed and presses a quick kiss to my lips. "I'll be back." His thumb caresses my cheek for a moment before he turns and walks toward the door. He stops, his hand resting on the door handle before he turns back to me. "This is just the beginning of us, Kate." He smiles that perfect smile at me. Straight white teeth, perfectly tanned skin. Mussed hair and muscles that look like they could burst through his shirt. He is the sexiest man I've ever laid eyes on…and he's mine.

"The beginning of us," I repeat sleepily. "I love you, Sam."

His tired face brightens at my admission to him. "I love you more," he replies, closing the door behind him. And he's right. This is just the beginning of our story. There will be many more chapters to come—happy and sad and everything in between. But at the end of the day, when we're old, I know I will look at him and know that we lived happily ever after.

EPILOGUE

"Are you sure you want me to come with you?" Kate asks as she rubs her hands together with lotion. I could watch her all day. Every move, every task is done with such grace.

"I wouldn't want to go if you weren't coming with me," I tell her.

"It's just..." She hesitates. "You haven't seen your brother since he left. And then there's Emilia, and I just feel awkward."

"Don't," I stop her. "Emilia is the past. She's Alex's wife, the mother to my niece. That's all she is. And Alex too, they are both dying to meet you."

She scrunches her nose up and lowers her eyes. "I'm not one to get jealous, but I just think it might be weird. What if seeing her brings up old feelings for you?" She frantically tosses clothes into a suitcase that sits on the end of her bed as a means of distraction.

"Kate. Would you please stop. I want you with me. I need you with me. There are no feelings for Emilia and never will be."

She puts on a gray t-shirt, pulling her long hair out from under the collar. God, I love her hair. Her long, beautiful hair.

Aside from the tumor, Kate was most worried about shaving part of her head for her surgery. The neurosurgeon was able to remove the tumor with a minimal incision, and you wouldn't even be able to locate the small area they needed to shave. Not that it would've mattered to me if they shaved her entire head. Everything about her is stunning.

"Why are you looking at me like that?" She laughs, wiggling into a pair of tight black skinny jeans. Even in jeans and a t-shirt, I find her to be the most beautiful woman in the world. Her sharp blue eyes stand out against her tanned skin and brown hair.

"Because I'm the luckiest guy in the world," I answer her. When I think about how much worse that tumor could've been, or the fact that I could've lost her in a moment's notice, my insides sink. She's it for me. I know this without a doubt in my mind.

She saunters across the room to me, wrapping her arms around my neck. "It's me who's lucky." She presses a soft kiss to my lips.

My arm snakes around her waist, pulling her closer to me. "I could kiss you all day, Kate. But if we don't leave right now, we'll never catch our flight."

She smiles against my lips and runs her hand over my groin. "Maybe we should just get undressed and get back into bed." She palms my dick, and I instantly grow hard.

"Kate," I groan into her mouth. "Tonight, I'm going to ravage you." I break our kiss and step back.

She mockingly grumbles at me, "Fine. But if Alex is a dick or if I hate Emilia, I'm getting a hotel." She cocks an eyebrow at me. I know she's on edge over meeting my brother, but mostly this is about Emilia. I hate that she feels the slightest bit of insecurity, but I need her to see that it's her that I love.

"Deal."

She slides her feet into a pair of Converse, grabs a black jacket, and her large travel purse. "Ready," she says with a smile. I pull our two suitcases out of her house and load them into my car while Kate locks up.

I moved into her house when she was released from the hospital. It made sense to be right there with her to help her with whatever she needed. Truth be told, once the tumor was removed and had relieved the pressure on her brain, she instantly snapped back and had very little side effects or recovery time. She met with therapists for a few weeks to ensure that she hadn't lost any mobility or speech functions, but like the little fighter she is, she got a clean bill of health and was released to normal activity after just a couple of months.

Kate returned to work part-time and has been careful not to overdo it. From all outward appearances, she's on the road to a full recovery. Of course, there's always a chance of reoccurrence, but the surgeon said it was highly unlikely. I've made it my job to gently nudge her and ensure she's getting her annual neurology checkups and stays healthy—because I intend to have her around forever.

The airport is always a zoo, and we barely make our plane, but once we're settled into our seats, Kate laces her fingers through mine, giving them a gentle squeeze. She rests her head on my shoulder and closes her eyes as we ascend, and a calmness settles through me. Everything I care about will be in one house, under one roof, in just a couple of hours.

I'm pulling luggage off the baggage carousel and Kate is pounding away on her phone when I see him across the terminal. I haven't seen Alex since he came to see me the day he left for Oregon. I was a mess, sitting on my couch, all shot up and no idea what my future was going to hold. He looks so different now, yet so much the same.

He always had my father's darker complexion, hair and eyes, and I always took after my mother. A bit lighter, more golden. So different for twins. He's dressed casually in a pair of dark jeans and a black button down shirt, sleeves rolled up to his elbows, and his hair is slightly longer than it used to be. More casual, carefree. Family life has suited him well. I want that. I need that.

He raises his hand in a wave when he sees me, and a giant smile spreads across his face as he approaches. I return his smile and instantly feel the anxiety I've been carrying around begin to settle. I don't know if I should reach out my hand for a handshake or if we're going to just greet each other with a 'hello', but as he stands in front of me, he instantly opens his arms for a hug, and I take it.

My brother. My other half. My first friend, and at one time, my fiercest enemy. We embrace for a moment with a few pats to each other's backs.

"Good to see ya, man," he says.

"Good to see you, too." I shrug out of his embrace, anxious to introduce Kate. When I turn to her, she's smiling at us, and I can tell her uneasiness has also settled—for now. "Alex, this is Kate. Kate, this is my brother, Alex."

Kate reaches out her hand to shake Alex's, but he pulls her in for a hug as well, and she laughs as he wraps his arms around her in a tight hug.

"How in the world my brother found you is beyond me." He

holds her out for a better look. "But he is one lucky hell of a guy."

Her cheeks blush, and Kate bursts out laughing and I do, too. Alex has instantly made us feel welcome and comfortable, and for that I'm grateful.

"Do you have all your bags?" he asks, reaching for Kate's bag.

"We do." I begin following him. A few minutes later, we're packed into a giant SUV and on our way to Alex's home.

"So we're on the coast," Alex tells Kate. I've already told her all of this, but she listens intently to Alex like it's the first time she's hearing this. "Right on the water. It's freezing most of the time, but it's beautiful. There are these sand dunes..." He carries on about the beach and how much he loves the peace and tranquility, and Kate smiles. He's such a different man than what I remember—a *good* different.

"And Gracie is a handful! She's almost walking now and all over the place," Alex speaks so lovingly of his daughter. This will be my first time meeting my niece. I have a million pictures of her, and she's the perfect blend of Alex and Emilia. She has soft pale skin, but dark hair and fiery eyes. Alex tells us she's a spitfire, which I believe with who both of her parents are.

"And you're going to love Emilia," Alex tells Kate, and I see her tense just a bit. "She's making a huge dinner. I wanted to go out so she didn't have to cook, but your first night here she wanted you both to relax and not feel pressured to go out for dinner. She has become quite the cook." He smiles at Kate before turning his eyes back to the road. He glances at me in the rearview mirror and I smile, grateful that we get to spend this time with my brother. It wasn't that long ago, I would've never envisioned this happening.

"Maybe we can catch up on that case you were working a

few months back. I'm curious to hear how that turned out," he says, his eyes curious. There he is, the brother who has let the criminal element go, but as we in law enforcement know, it's never really gone. He may have turned his life around, thank the good Lord. But he's Alex Estrada Cortez, that life will always be in him. Of course he's talking about Navarro's case. Alex was critical in providing key information I was able to use to assist in bringing Jesus Navarro into custody.

"Sounds good."

"Emilia is anxious to show you both the coffee shop, too. She's expanded it into a small bookstore as well."

"I love books!" Kate exclaims.

Alex's lips twist into a smile. "She has a decent selection. She started out as a coffee shop and internet café," he starts. "But we outgrew that. We needed more space. There is a new community college in town, and the shop quickly became the place where everyone came to study or relax. When the business next door closed, she bought it and built out, adding more seating and a small bookstore. I'm so goddamn proud of her. She has vision where I saw nothing," he comments, and I grin. Alex was always about starting new. He never could look at something old, something worn, and see the beauty in it. I'm glad Emilia has that vision.

"Can't wait to see it," I remark, a look of pride shows in his eyes.

Thirty minutes later, we're pulling into the driveway of a beautiful big house. It's large but not massive. Beautiful but not overstated. The front door swings open and there stands Emilia bobbing a little girl on her hip.

My heart leaps when I see the two of them, a flood of emotions bubbling to the surface. Kate looks over her shoulder at me and offers me a worrisome smile.

"There's my girls," Alex sighs as he closes the car door and opens the back of the SUV. He pulls our luggage down, and Gracie squeals in Emilia's arms. Alex and I pull the luggage toward the front door, stopping just outside. Emilia hands Gracie to Alex and reaches out for Kate, pulling her into a gentle embrace.

"Welcome, Kate. I'm so glad I finally get to meet you." Emilia's eyes meet mine, and she offers me a sweet smile.

"I'm so glad to be here," Kate responds and steps back, a look of nervousness etched across her face.

"Sam," Emilia says, wrapping her arms around me next, and I instantly relax. There are no feelings to battle, no ghosts from the past lurking and waiting to find me. I feel a general sense of relief at Emilia's embrace. "Thank you for coming."

"I'm glad we were finally able to make it work." I reach out for Kate's hand and she takes it. A small smile pulls at the corner of her lips, and she casts her eyes downward. She's fine. The awkwardness she was expecting is not there. The ice is broken, and we can all relax now.

Just inside the door we're welcomed into an enormous foyer. A large, ornate crystal chandelier hangs from the tall, coffered ceiling. Alex hands the baby back to Emilia, and she guides us into the kitchen.

Alex disappears with our luggage, leaving Kate and myself in the kitchen with Emilia and Gracie.

Emilia does what she does best, making everyone feel welcome and comfortable. "Anyone want a drink? Wine? Beer? Water? Soda?"

"I'd love a glass of wine," Kate responds. "White if you have it."

Emilia's lips twist into a grin. "White is my favorite." Good. Something they have in common.

Emilia hands Gracie to Kate and walks across the kitchen, opens a door, and steps inside. I realize it's a small wine cellar. Of course, my brother would have a wine cellar in his house. I shake my head and chuckle to myself.

I catch Kate out of the corner of my eye, bouncing Gracie in her arms. She slowly presses her lips to my niece's sweet head and something inside me softens. I see my future with Kate standing right here in this kitchen. Family. Kids. Happiness. My heart is momentarily overwhelmed, and I fight back a growing lump in my throat.

"Pinot Grigio okay?" Emilia asks when she emerges from the wine cellar with a bottle in her hand.

"Perfect," Kate answers, grinning at me.

"Good. I made a butternut squash ravioli with brown butter sauce for dinner. Pinot will go perfectly with it." Emilia uncorks the bottle and lets it sit for a moment on the counter while she pulls down wine glasses.

I expected to be uneasy around her, but I'm not. She moves flawlessly through the kitchen, and I search for what I saw in her years ago, coming up empty. Not bad, just empty. Everything I thought I believed I wanted then, I don't. Everything I want is standing in front of me, holding my sweet niece.

"Sam, can you help me with the salad?" Emilia asks, setting four wine glasses on the large, quartz covered kitchen island.

"Yeah." I snap out of my thoughts and walk over to the island where a large cutting board sits with a variety of vegetables on it.

"Everything has been washed, can you slice the peppers and cucumbers? I'll manage the tomatoes." She pours four glasses of wine and puts one down in front of me. I pick up the knife and core the yellow and red pepper, slicing them into evenly sliced portions.

"So how was the flight?" Emilia asks, handing a glass of wine to Kate, who's still holding Gracie.

"It was good. Quick," I answer her and watch Kate sip some wine and walk with the baby over to a large set of floor to ceiling bay windows. Kate is talking softly to the baby, and both of them look out over the backyard that leads to the sand dunes and then to the beach.

Slicing cucumbers, Emilia sips wine and dices tomatoes on another cutting board next to me.

"I can't even tell you how excited Alex has been that you guys were coming. He's been pacing the house all morning, making sure everything was all set." She laughs and looks at me. Her hazel eyes crinkle at the corners when she smiles and, while she's beautiful, she's nothing compared to Kate.

"You did not have to do anything special for us, Em," I tell her.

"We didn't." She shrugs. "Just freshened the sheets on the bed in the guest room and grocery shopped. Alex said he wants to make enchiladas, your mom's recipe or something." She tosses the sliced tomatoes into a giant bowl of chopped lettuce sitting in the center of the island.

"She made the best enchiladas," I remark quietly, remembering the meals my mom used to make for us. My heart aches we didn't get to spend more time with her, but I find comfort in how she used mealtime to bring us together as a family.

"She did," Alex responds as he steps back into the kitchen and reaches for the last glass of wine on the counter. "I still miss her," he says somberly, and that lump that had disappeared is finding its way back.

"I do, too," I admit and clear my throat, choking back my emotions. All of this is overwhelming. I never expected to be back on good terms with my brother and have some semblance of an extended family again. This is what my mom would want, though. Alex and I were her life, and I know she's smiling down on us right now.

Emilia breaks up the somber mood. "So anyway, shredded beef enchiladas, rice, and Mexican street corn for dinner another night!" Alex glances at me, and something unsaid passes between us. Common ground. The love we both share for our mother.

We all fall into easy conversation, snacking on cheese, crackers, and wine. Kate is absolutely in love with Gracie and has a hard time giving her back to Emilia. My heart is at peace watching her with Gracie. Emilia invites Kate to help get Gracie ready for bed, and Kate jumps at the chance. When the girls disappear, Alex and I get some time to catch up alone.

"Let's go out back." Alex gestures to the French doors that lead out to the back patio. Alex lights a gas fire pit in the center of the stone patio that's surrounded by plush outdoor furniture. Alex and I sit opposite each other with newly topped off glasses of wine. The wind is picking up and the fire feels good, warming the air around the cooling ocean breeze.

"So tell me about Navarro," Alex says, propping his foot up over his opposite knee.

"We got him," I start, twirling the wine glass in my right hand. "I don't think we would've gotten him that fast if you hadn't tipped us off to the strip clubs. We didn't know he was moving money through those."

Alex laughs, "Seriously? How did you not know that?"

"I don't know, man." I shake my head, feeling a little dumb that we hadn't picked up on that sooner. Most criminal organizations pass money through semi-legitimate business fronts.

"Always look at strip clubs, night clubs, those shady used car lots—many of them are a front," he offers.

I nod my head, tucking that info away. "So anyway, there are over one hundred criminal counts against him and those arrested with him. The FBI, DEA, and ATF were able to present charges."

"Daaamn." He cringes.

"Anyway, on to the next. But seriously, Alex. I know you left all of that behind you, but I really appreciate your help."

He smiles warmly. "Anything for you, brother."

Changing the conversation to something more upbeat, I say, "So tell me how you're doing."

"Good, good. Just managing the business. Picking up the slack with Gracie while Em is at the café."

"You have a beautiful family, Alex. I'm proud of you." And I mean it.

"I love them more than I thought was humanly possible," he admits, leaning closer to the fire. It's easy to see the love he has for Emilia and Gracie and how much those two have changed his life for the better—to the man he was always meant to be.

"I can see that." I turn and see Emilia and Kate standing at the kitchen island, smiling and laughing, and my heart is happy and content.

The sun is barely rising when I sneak out of the room to let Kate get some extra sleep. We didn't exactly go to sleep last night, and I know she's tired. As I descend the stairs, I see Emilia rocking Gracie in an oversized recliner, and I can hear Gracie cooing.

"Good morning," Emilia says as she sees me approaching. "You're up early."

I shrug. "I've always been an early riser." I lean in and press a kiss to Gracie's sweet little head before throwing myself down on the couch.

"Can you take her for a few minutes?" Emilia asks, setting the little girl in my arms regardless of my answer. "I just want to get some coffee started and pop a breakfast casserole in the oven. She likes to be held and snuggled in the morning and who's better to do that than her uncle?"

I cradle my sweet niece in my arms, a blanket covering her little body. She smiles at me, and I press a kiss to her chubby little cheek. She settles into my arms and rests her head on my chest. Her dark hair falls across her forehead, and she coos as I gently rock her.

I can hear Emilia behind me in the kitchen, and I settle into plush couch, leaning onto the arm and snuggling Gracie.

"You look like a natural," Alex says quietly as he comes down the stairs, joining me in the living room.

Gracie lifts her head and smiles at her dad, but sets her head right back down on my chest as he settles into a large recliner.

"I can't say I've honestly ever held a baby before," I remark.

Alex chuckles. "Well, she's beyond the little baby stage, but she still likes to be held like one." He smiles affectionately at Gracie and looks up at me. "Kate still sleeping?"

I nod as Emilia joins us back in the living room, carrying a cup of coffee for both Alex and me. She sets mine on the coffee table, just within reach, and Alex takes his. "I like her," Emilia says, returning with her own cup of coffee. "I don't know what I was expecting," she admits. "But it wasn't Kate. She's the real deal." Emilia slides into Alex's lap on the recliner, carefully juggling her cup of coffee.

"She is," I tell them. "I wasn't looking for anyone, and she just kind of showed up and never left."

"You moved into her house, asshole," Alex laughs.

I correct him, "Her guesthouse."

"Regardless, I like her. She's good for you. She's smart, gorgeous, but mostly, she's got a good heart. I can tell."

Emilia nods in agreement. "So is it serious?" he asks, tiptoeing around the question I know they're both wanting to ask me.

"It is." I pat Gracie's chest and look at her sweet fingers gripping my t-shirt. "She's definitely the one. I even—" I pause, stopping myself.

"What?" Emilia looks at me, prodding for more detail.

"Nothing." I decide to keep this to myself. My pulse quickens when I think of the diamond ring I have hidden in my luggage upstairs. Emilia notices my hesitation and moves on.

"And I would never have known she had surgery," she says, looking up at the stairs to make sure Kate isn't coming down into a conversation about her. "I was worried when you told us she had a brain tumor removed."

I blow out a puff of air. "I know. It was a scary time for us, but I wasn't ready to lose her." I think back to that time in our lives. Kate means everything to me. She's the one I want to talk to first thing in the morning and the one I want to kiss goodnight. Good days, bad days, and boring days in between, she's the one I want by my side.

"Well, I'm happy for you, brother," Alex says, sipping his coffee. "She'll fit right into this family."

I nod, thinking of Kate being a Cortez. "I believe she will, too."

An hour later and Kate is still sleeping so I decide to take a walk on the beach. Dressed in a sweatshirt and joggers, I head out the back patio.

Emilia is hot on my tail. "Mind if I join you?" she asks, pulling her long hair up into a ponytail that sways from side to side in the wind.

"Sure."

She guides me down the stone paved trail, off of their property, and beyond the dunes to the gorgeous beach. The area outside their house has been mostly cleaned, but just beyond that lies large pieces of driftwood, and we maneuver around those.

"So how are you feeling?" Emilia asks once we get out closer to the water. "How are you really feeling?" She shoots me a look, and I know she's talking about my recovery from the shooting.

I glance at her out of the corner of my eye, thinking back to how this once shy, nervous girl has blossomed into a beautiful woman so full of life and ambition. "I'm actually doing really well. No lie."

"Good. I know that it's not easy to bounce back from an injury like that, and then when Alex told me you were transferring to Los Angeles, I felt like maybe it was too soon." I can see the genuine concern in her eyes.

I shrug, stuffing my hands in the pockets of my sweatshirt. "I wasn't running, Emilia. I was just looking to start over. A clean slate."

She looks at me, her lips twisting into a concerned smile. "If anyone deserves it, it's you, Sam."

We walk quietly down the beach, the water lapping near our

feet. We come across only one other person, an old man walking his equally as old Golden Retriever, who runs right up to Emilia and jumps on her. She laughs, tossing her head back and rubs the graying dog behind its ears.

"Jefferson." She giggles, and he jumps down.

"Damn dog has no manners, does he?" the old man barks when he finally catches up.

"Hey, Mr. Watkins," Emilia says, leaning in to give the man a hug.

"Good morning to you, too, doll," he says, embracing Emilia warmly.

She nods to me. "This is my brother-in-law, Sam Cortez. He's visiting us for a few days from Los Angeles."

"Nice to meet you, son. Los Angeles is a shit hole, isn't it?" He reaches out his hand to shake mine. "Never could figure out why everyone wants to live in that fishbowl of a town." He carries on about how horrible Los Angeles is, the traffic, the smog, and the horrible people.

Emilia rolls her eyes, and we laugh at Mr. Watkins. Emilia sends Jefferson and Mr. Watkins on their way, turning around every so often to make sure he made it back home to the small old beach house that sits beyond their house.

"So I'm thinking about proposing to Kate," I say, catching Emilia off guard.

She stops dead in her tracks and looks at me. "What?" she asks with a grin. "Are you serious? When?"

"Here," I tell her. "While we're here."

"Oh my gosh!" Her hand flies up to cover her mouth. "Do you even have a ring? Do you know how you're going to do it?" She's asking so many questions that I can't keep up, and all I can do is laugh at her. "Can I help you?" She bounces excitedly in the hard sand.

I stare out at the ocean, pondering my decision and it just feels like it's supposed to happen now. "I didn't know how I was going to do it, or where—but it just seems right to do it while we're here. We've been through so much, so quickly, and the timing just seems right." I shrug a single shoulder and look at Emilia. "And I'd love your help."

"Oh my god, Sam." She shakes her head. "What about this?" She taps her lips with her pointer finger. "We have reservations tonight at Molina's in town." She points her finger at me. "Don't do it there, it's too cliché'." She grins conspiratorially behind us at their sprawling house down the beach. "But I ordered a dessert assortment from the local bakery in town, and it's being delivered to the house today. I was planning to have dessert back at the house with wine on the enclosed patio after dinner. We have these amazing lights and a fireplace, and it would be perfect. It's comfortable and private and—"

"That sounds perfect," I laugh at her, appreciating her enthusiasm. However, I can tell I've lost her. Her mind is going a million miles an hour.

Emilia snaps out of her thoughts. "We need to get back to the house." I can see her wheels turning again, and she turns around and takes off in the direction of the house. I follow closely behind her, but she's already pulled a cell phone out of her jacket pocket and she's talking to someone. I hear the words 'flowers' and 'champagne', and I look at Emilia who has a permanent smile on her face. I appreciate her help because I've been so goddamn nervous about this proposal that having Emilia think of flowers and champagne is appreciated.

As we approach the house, she turns to me. "I'm just getting dessert and some flowers for the patio. I don't want to overstep...this is all yours, understand?" She grabs both of my arms with her hands, excitedly biting her lip. "And if you don't want me to do that, tell me to stop."

I shake my head and chuckle at my sister-in-law. It's the first time I've thought of her that way, as my sister-in-law, Alex's wife, and not as Emilia, the girl I thought I once wanted.

"That sounds perfect, Em. Thank you for your help."

When we step back inside the house, I find Kate feeding Gracie baby food in a high chair and drinking coffee. Her hair is twisted into a pile on top of her head, and she's still wearing her pajamas. She looks comfortable, at home, and this makes me more than happy.

"Seriously, you're going to have our guests care for our kid," Emilia says to Alex, jokingly annoyed.

Alex is sitting on the kitchen island, looking at his phone. Kate and I laugh, and Emilia shakes her head.

"I wanted to feed Gracie," Kate says. "He was taking perfectly good care of this little nugget." She taps Gracie's nose with the baby spoon ever so gently. Gracie giggles and Kate melts. "When I came downstairs, I found Alex sitting with her, and I asked to take over. I cannot believe how late I slept. I must've been tired."

"Travel will do that to you," Alex says, sliding off the counter. He plants a giant kiss on Em's lips, and I grab another cup of coffee.

"I'm going to need you to run a few errands for me," Emilia says to Alex as she pulls a small stack of plates down from a cupboard. "And I'm wondering if you'd go with him, Kate?"

Kate freezes, looking to me suspiciously and then back to Emilia, swallowing hard. I can see she's unsettled by Emilia's request. I shoot her a reassuring look. "Um, sure."

Emilia gives Kate the most disarming smile. "I just need to get a few things done around here, and I have a very specific list and I know for a fact Alex won't get it right." Alex feigns shock, and she continues, unfazed. "I'm putting together a charcuterie board for us to snack off of this afternoon. I need a nice selection of cheeses, aged, firm, soft, creamy, and meats. I need more than just salami." She raises her eyebrows at Alex, and he rolls his eyes.

"Prosciutto and sausage would be great. And don't forget pickles, olives, peppers, and some nuts," Emilia continues to rattle off. "And an assortment of crackers and bread, and, oh, some apples and grapes and figs, and some jam and maybe some dried fruits, too." She grins once she's finished.

Alex's eyes bulge, and Emilia turns a look to Kate. "See, this is why I need you, Kate. I just have too much to do here at the house, and Alex will never get this right." Emilia smiles at Kate, and Kate seems to relax. "And you," Emilia points at me. "You're on babysitting duty."

"I can handle this," Kate responds, standing up from the table. She hands me the spoon that she was feeding Gracie with and carries her empty coffee mug to Emilia, who is now standing at the sink. "Let me go get ready and I'll make sure we get everything." Kate disappears and Alex waits a moment before he speaks up softly.

"That sounded awfully like you're trying to get rid of me and Kate." He looks between Emilia and me.

"I am!" she whisper yells. "I have some shit to do and Sam's going to help me, and it's a surprise, and I just need you to not ask any more questions and do as I say." This fierceness is what I remember loving about Emilia. When she sets her mind to something, nothing or nobody will get in her way.

"Alright, boss. How long do I need to keep her occupied?" he asks, glancing at the time on his phone and back to Emilia.

"A couple of hours. Take her to the café first. Kill some time showing her around downtown."

Alex makes a face. "Downtown is one single city block, Emilia."

I actually laugh at Alex's reaction.

"Do you think I don't know this?" she snaps at him, looking ready to throttle him. "Just kill some damn time."

"Whatever this surprise is, it better be good," he mutters, pushing himself off the island and walking toward Gracie and me. He bends down and presses a kiss to the top of Gracie's head before looking at me. "Her diaper needs to be changed." He grins. "Upstairs is the changing table." He smacks my shoulder and disappears as Emilia busts out laughing.

"You heard your brother. Go change her diaper." Emilia wipes down a large wood board and pulls small cheese knives from a drawer, setting them on the island next to the board.

I shake my head at my niece. "You hear that, kid? They're making me change your diaper."

Gracie just grins at me, showing me all four of her teeth. With a resigned sigh, I pull her carefully from her highchair and toss Emilia a dirty look as I take Gracie to get changed.

Six hours later, we're all sitting around a table in a dimly lit, quaint Italian restaurant. We've just eaten the most amazing meal ever, and now we're all enjoying a glass of wine. Kate's hand is wrapped firmly in mine, and while I should be a bundle of nerves right now, I'm oddly at peace.

My mind keeps wandering back to the house where Emilia pulled off a small miracle in a matter of hours. Desserts were delivered, along with various bouquets of flowers. She strung little white lights to add some additional mood lighting to the patio, and she left strict instructions for the babysitter to get the fireplace started right about...now. I glance at my watch.

Emilia nods to Alex, who takes care of the bill, and we all collect our jackets as we wait for the car to be brought up from the valet.

"I cannot thank you enough for this amazing dinner," Kate graciously thanks Alex and Emilia. "And the charcuterie and wine before was amazing."

"That is thanks to you," Emilia chuckles, giving Alex the side eye.

"I would have been fine with packaged pepperoni." Alex shrugs, and we all laugh. My nerves finally kick in , and my hands begin to sweat. I haven't been able to keep my eyes off of Kate tonight, and I plan to bury myself in her later after she's wearing the ring I picked out. Kate naked with nothing on but my ring is all I can think about.

"And this is why I asked Kate to go with you!" Emilia slides her hand into Alex's just as the car arrives, snapping me out of my thoughts. Alex drives us home, pointing out little historical markers throughout town as we head back to the house.

Emilia damn near runs ahead of us to get into the house first under the ruse that she needs to use the restroom. I know she's making sure everything is set up and nothing will spoil this proposal. I pat the pocket on my suit coat, making sure the velvet box is still in place. Swallowing against my dry throat, I realize I'm minutes away from asking Kate to be my wife.

Kate leans on me and I press a kiss to her lips as we stand just outside the front door. "I'm having a really nice time," she says, her eyes shimmering in the moonlight. "I'm really glad I came."

"I told you everything was going to be just fine." I knew that as soon as Kate met Alex and Emilia that everything would fall into place. And it did.

She nods and smiles. "I know. I really like Emilia and Alex, they make me feel comfortable."

"I knew you would." I give her another quick kiss, and we head inside.

Kate kicks off her heels and turns to me. "I'm going to get changed and get out of this dress." She tugs at the fitted black dress that highlights every curve on her body.

Emilia overhears and says, "Sounds perfect. Meet us out on the porch when you come back down. I have some dessert out there for us."

"Sounds great." Kate leaves us behind to get changed while Emilia and I head back to the enclosed patio where a fire roars in the fireplace, casting warmth throughout. Emilia has outdone herself. Flowers sit in various bouquets throughout the patio, providing just a touch of elegance to an already beautiful space. Little shimmering lights twinkle from where Emilia has carefully strung them around indoor trees, and they provide a romantic ambiance to the patio. I pace the patio, mumbling to myself over and over as my pulse quickens knowing she's on her way back down here and I'm about to drop to my knee.

The patio is lined with floor to ceiling windows that open or close depending on the weather, that look out over the ocean and beach. Although at night, you can only see hints of the water from the moonlight. Alex tosses himself down onto a loveseat and kicks his feet up on a chest that doubles as a coffee table.

Alex still has no idea that I'm about to propose. He's clueless as he sits and tries to talk football with me. Of course, I'm nervous as hell, trying to remember what I'm going to say, and the Pittsburgh Steelers are the last thing on my mind. Emilia, on the other hand, is a nervous wreck, running all over, tweaking little things here and there, setting out dessert, and finally uncorking a new bottle of wine until she finally collapses into a chair next to Alex.

"Where is she?" Emilia asks just above a whisper, seemingly more nervous than me.

I chuckle and shake my head.

"Relax," Alex says, rubbing Emilia's leg. "She wanted to change. Speaking of which, I think I'm going to go get—"

"Sit down!" Emilia orders abruptly, and Alex looks at her like she's lost her damn mind.

"What has gotten into you, woman?" he asks with a laugh.

Her eyes widen in seriousness as she tries to lower her voice. "Something important is about to happen, and you're going to sit your ass right there and not move." She grasps his arm, and he settles back in eyeing me suspiciously.

Alex looks back and forth between me and Emilia, and suddenly begins to piece everything together. He notices the flowers, the lights, and his eyes widen. "Now? Right now? Tonight?"

I nod, trying to swallow against my dry throat, and my nerves have finally gotten the better of me. I can feel my face begin to flush, my heart race, and my hands begin to shake.

"She's coming," Emilia whispers just as Kate comes bounding into the room in a pair of black leggings and an oversized cream sweater. Her wavy hair falls over her shoulders, and she smiles softly at me as she approaches.

We're all silent, staring back at her with grins pasted on our faces, and Kate starts to look around between all three of us.

"What's going on?" she asks, thinking something is wrong. I can see the nervousness written across her face.

I take a step toward her, closing the distance. "Kate..." My voice shakes, and I take a deep breath. "The very moment I saw you behind your house that day, I knew in my heart that I wanted to be with you forever." My voice breaks, and Kate's eyes fill with tears. She knows. This is it. "Before you even said a word, before you shook my hand in that backyard, my soul looked into yours and I knew you were 'home' to me. Every day since then, I've only fallen more in love with you. Every day I wake up and can't envision my life without you in it."

Kate's hands are now covering her mouth, and her entire body shakes as I speak. Emilia holds Alex's hand as they both watch us, and a tear slips from Emilia's eye and rolls down her cheek. I take another deep breath and try to steady my voice as I drop to my knee and pull a small velvet box out of the pocket of my jacket.

"Kate Stevens," my voice continues to shake, "will you marry me?"

The tears finally fall from her eyes, and she collapses to her knees in front of me as I fumble with the box. She's nodding her head frantically and finally musters up the word I've been praying she'd say.

"Yes," she gasps. "Yes. Yes. Yes. I'd marry you a million times." She extends her left hand that is also shaking uncontrollably, and I slide the round diamond that used to be my mother's onto her finger. My aunt and uncle have been holding onto this ring since she died. It was an emotional night when I flew back to Phoenix to retrieve it, but I'm so thankful they've held onto it for all these years. There is no one that is more deserving of my mother's ring than Kate.

Alex notices the ring and his eyes mist over. So many days we spent apart, broken by lies, bound by deceit, and betrayed by the man who had created this family. Only in the end, we rose above and came out stronger—together as family.

ALSO BY REBECCA SHEA

Bound & Broken Series

Broken by Lies – Book 1

Bound by Lies -Book 2

Betrayed by Lies - Book 3

Unbreakable Series

Unbreakable -Book 1

Undone -Book 2

Unforgiven - Book 3

Standalone Tiles

Dare Me

Fault Lines

Unexpectedly Yours

Always Been You

Hollywood Chronicles

co-written with A.L. Jackson

One Wild Night

One Wild Ride

CONNECT WITH REBECCA SHEA

Website
www.rebeccasheaauthor.com

Sign up for Rebecca Shea's newsletter
http://tinyurl.com/h8mfya2

Sign up for Rebecca Shea's new release and sale alerts
http://www.subscribepage.com/j1m3c5

Follow Rebecca Shea on Facebook:
www.facebook.com/rebeccasheaauthor

Follow Rebecca Shea on Instagram:
https://www.instagram.com/rebeccasheaauthor/

Email: rebeccasheaauthor@gmail.com